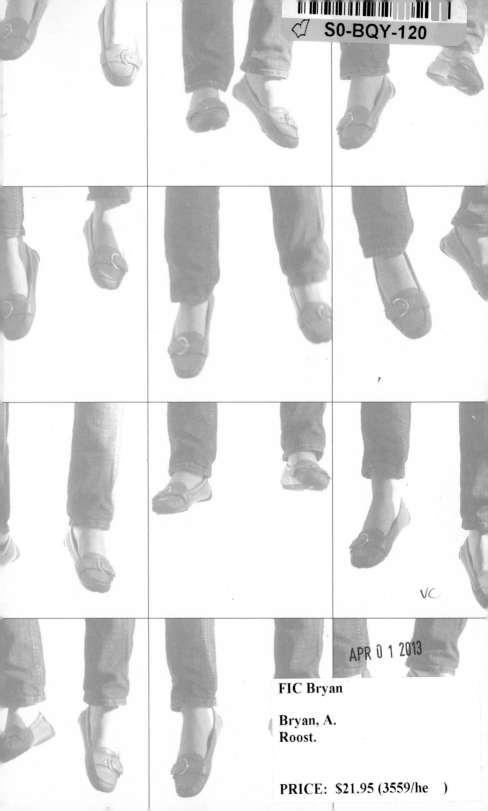

roost

roost

a novel

ALI BRYAN

FREEHAND BOOKS

Ali Bryan 2013

Canada Council   Conseil des Arts
for the Arts   du Canada

Freehand Books gratefully acknowledges the support of the Canada Council for the Arts for its publishing program. ¶ Freehand Books, an imprint of Broadview Press Inc., acknowledges the financial support for its publishing program provided by the Government of Canada through the Canada Book Fund.

Freehand Books
515 – 815 1st Street SW   Calgary, Alberta   T2P 1N3
www.freehand-books.com

Book orders: LitDistCo
100 Armstrong Avenue   Georgetown, Ontario   L7G 5S4
Telephone: 1-800-591-6250   Fax: 1-800-591-6251
orders@litdistco.ca
www.litdistco.ca

Library and Archives Canada Cataloguing In Publication

Bryan, Ali, 1978–
Roost / Ali Bryan.

Issued also in electronic formats.
ISBN 978-1-55481-137-3

I. Title.

PS8603.R885R66 2013   C813'.6   C2012-907093-9

Edited by Robyn Read
Book design and cover photography by Natalie Olsen, kisscutdesign.com
Author photo by Phil Crozier, PHOTOPHILCRO

Printed on FSC recycled paper and bound in Canada

for
Pippa
Hugo
Odessa

"Claudia, we need matches!" my father hollers from the dining room.

"I'm getting them!"

I'm standing on a chair, searching through the cupboard above the kitchen sink. Behind the vitamins and piping bags, I find a lighter from when I used to smoke, from a previous life. It is off-white with a red thing that looks like a guillotine, and because I no longer smoke, its only purpose is to light birthday candles. Fat ones shaped like numbers and the ones that never blow out. When I reach for it a tube of Polysporin falls on my head and then lands in the sink full of cold, cloudy water and a few floating pieces of omelette. I'll fish it out later. Back in the dining room they've already started singing "Happy Birthday." Tonight we're celebrating my mother's sixtieth.

"Just wait!" I shield the flames as I set down the cake in front of her. But no one waits. They finish singing and, with her hands braced against the bevelled edge of my unfashionable oak table, she blows mightily. Some candles extinguish immediately, while others, the kind that do not blow out, persistently flicker, making her sweat. Her grandchildren have abandoned their seats and converged on the cake, but they have the wind power of hamsters and do little more than spray the surface with microscopic bits of the snack mix they spent most of the night gorging on. Four pieces of untouched lasagna on side plates remain on the table as if waiting to be taste-tested.

Two of the kids are mine. Wesley is four. His Transformers underwear, which is on inside out, peeks above the waistband of his jogging pants.

"Sit back," I say. "Give Grandma some space."

He returns to his chair obligingly, but he stands instead of sits, keeping his gaze on the trick candles and fantasizing over which piece of the cake will be his. He rubs at his red upper lip and nostrils. My older brother Dan looks at him, repulsed.

"What?" I say defensively. "He has impetigo. He's itchy."

"I didn't say anything," he replies, as my mother makes a second grand attempt to blow out her cake.

"No, but you looked at him like he was disgusting."

"I did not look at him like he was disgusting."

My mother gives Dan and me a beseeching look.

"Come on, Wes." I take his hand and lead him off his chair. "Go wash your hands." He saunters out of the room and across the hall to the bathroom. "Try not to touch your face," I call after him.

Two candles remain lit. "Just take them off and throw them in something," my father says impatiently, pushing a can of Sprite towards my mother. But it's a full can and she can't waste it, so he sighs and puts them out with his wet fingers. I am certain some of his saliva has landed on the cake.

At two and a half, Joan is my youngest. She has weaselled her way up onto my mom's lap and to her delight is served the first piece of birthday cake. Aside from occasionally humping things and believing that we are all engaged in an ongoing game of chase, she's the easier of my two children. She is less sensitive than Wes and more independent, and though this offers me some parental reprieve it also worries me; two-year-olds should need their mommies. They should cling to their legs and crawl into their beds and want help getting dressed.

"Come here, Joan." I gently slap my thigh, but she ignores me and begins licking her plate.

Dan refuses cake and quietly assists his daughter in eating hers. His wife, Allison-Jean, sits to his left. She's almost seven months pregnant, though she was fat to begin with. It will be their third child. Her hair is limp and the colour of lake trout, and she may have poor taste in shoes and a hyphenated name, but she can move people to tears when she plays the piano.

"Allison-Jean?" my mother says, offering her a lopsided piece of cake.

She accepts it to be nice and this pleases my mother, who all of a sudden looks weary.

"I'll have one," I say.

"There's a shocker," Dan says, grinning. He wipes the corners of his daughter Hannah's mouth with a Hello Kitty napkin that he then folds into a triangle. His family life is orderly. Structure over chaos, positive reinforcement over yelling. Weekend theme nights and regular bedtimes. On Fridays they play board games as a family and build puzzles with no missing pieces, and when they finish them they disassemble them and put the pieces back in their boxes, which look new because their kids have never tried to stand on them or jab them with tent pegs.

In my house, my grotty three-bed, two-bath bungalow, everything is missing a piece. Kleenex boxes are dented, towels are frayed, and the blinds are twisted like rebar. There is not enough suction in the vacuum, too much water pressure in the bathroom sink, and today there are too many people. After a quick survey of the dining room, I realize my dad has left the table.

I walk through the kitchen that opens out into the living

room. My father's at the back of the living room sliding the glass door that leads to the back deck open and shut.

"What are you doing?"

With one hand he takes off his glasses, while with the other he reaches up to the track above. "It's a bit jammed," he says. "See this thingamajig here? It should be lined up with this piece over here." He grunts as he points to it. "Do you have a Phillips head?"

"Yes, but you don't have to do this now."

"It will just take a minute."

"Seriously, it's not that bad," I argue. "I barely use that door."

But he spreads his arms across it anyway, grips the edges, and in a rocking motion pops it off the track. The weight causes him to stumble back.

"Whoa!" he says, catching his balance. He takes a few recovering steps forward, props the door against its stationary partner, and asks where he can find the toolbox.

"Is it time for presents?" Wes asks, poking at the small accumulation of gifts on the kitchen counter with a skewer.

"Give me that," I say, tossing the skewer in the junk drawer. "I think presents are a great idea." And I let him carry one of the least breakable-looking gifts into the dining room.

Dan and Allison-Jean both rise; she clears the dishes, while Dan follows Wes's lead and ferries the rest of the gifts into the dining room and assembles them into a neat pile on the table. My dad shuffles back to join us but doesn't sit down. I'm hoping the gift opening goes speedily so he can get back to fixing the door.

"Isn't it lovely, Gerald?" my mother says, holding up a teapot adorned with the characters from *The Wizard of Oz*.

My father nods.

"What does it do?" Dan asks, confused.

"What do you mean, what does it do? It's a teapot," I reply.

"Yes," my mother quickly intervenes, examining the jewelled appliqués on Dorothy's ruby slippers, "and I will use it the next time the ladies come to play bridge."

My father rushes my mother along. "Open the next one," he suggests.

"She collects teapots," I tell my brother.

"I do," my mother agrees, latching onto the next present. She moves briskly, tearing the paper on her gifts instead of carefully pulling back the tape, seemingly on board to get it over and done with. She opens a fancy cheese grater, a pair of leather gloves, and a picture, which she unearths from a sea of mauve tissue.

"What is it?" Wes asks, staring at the brown paper on the back of the frame.

"It's . . . it's my mother," she whispers. "It's a picture of my mother." She stares at it for some time before flipping it over for the group to admire. "But how did you . . . I mean it was ripped and bent and . . . I mean, look at it," my mother says. She turns it back over and runs her fingers over the glass. Dan points to Allison-Jean.

"It wasn't all me," she protests. "It was actually Daniel's idea."

"Yes, but you made it happen," he says dotingly.

She blushes. "You'd be surprised what they can do now to restore old photos."

"Well, yes. I am surprised," my mother says.

"Let me see," I say abruptly.

My mother delicately hands over the frame. I don't recognize the photo. I hardly even remember my grandmother and what I do recall of her does not correspond with the woman in the picture, who has a boyish figure and sculpted hair, who is wearing a dropped waist dress and long beads. In fact all I remember is her shortbread and her attic and how as she got older she looked increasingly like an amphibian.

"There's one more thing in there," Dan says, setting the dishevelled bag upright.

Of course there is, I think.

Dan waves my father back from the living room as my mother fishes through even more tissue paper. She pulls out an envelope and turns it over as though looking for instructions.

"What is it?" Wes asks impatiently.

"Open it up, Janice," my dad urges.

My mother tears open the edges. Allison-Jean frantically removes her camera from its Neoprene diaper of a case. Her children smile before she's even turned the camera on. Dan has repositioned himself behind my mother and appears to be sucking in his stomach. The level of anticipation in the room is compromising my ability to behave. I pick at Wes's abandoned piece of cake. My mother reads some sort of printed document and then puts her hand to her chest.

"Danny, you shouldn't have!"

This time I'm the one who asks, "What is it?"

"It's a trip to Cuba for your father and me!"

"Thanks for the heads-up," I mutter to Dan.

Dan ignores me. "You said for a long time you wanted to go to one of those all-inclusive resorts like your friend Betty Jane, so Allison-Jean talked to Dad and, well, you only turn sixty once."

My mother stands and hugs Dan and Allison-Jean from across the table, and I don't know whether to start singing "Kumbaya" or stick a fork in my eye.

"I thought you always wanted to go to Paris?"

My dad excuses himself once again to go work on the door.

"Open mine, Grandma!" Wes hollers, handing my mother a mysterious package wrapped in a damp hand towel from the bathroom.

"Oh my," she says, surprised. "I wonder what it could be."

He waits anxiously as my mother unfolds the towel. It smells like mildew and 1977, but no one dares to comment.

"Oh they are great, Wesley," my mother praises him, flipping through a stack of freshly drawn pictures of stick people with excessively large eyeballs, one of which has been drawn over my MasterCard bill. "Just lovely."

I get up from the table and disappear into my bedroom where I play Facebook Scrabble and quietly regret my inadequate gift. When I return to the kitchen, apologizing and waving around my phone, so that everyone knows I had important business matters to take care of, the sink's emptied, the dishes have been put in the dishwasher. I check; they were rinsed first. Allison-Jean and Dan are at the front door putting shoes on their kids. Mom and Dad join us.

"Do you need a bag, Mom?" I ask, looking past her and seeing her presents still on the dining room table.

"Oh. Yes, please."

I go and get her a grocery bag and she carefully slips her gifts inside.

My dad pats me on the back. "It's all done," he says proudly, referring to the sliding door.

"Thanks." I manage a smile.

The rest of the adults linger in the front foyer discussing Cuba.

"We leave tomorrow!" my mother reminds herself.

I open the door. It's mild outside. The air is damp, the stars not visible. A foghorn bellows from the bottom of the hill. The bass call of a container ship galumphing into Halifax harbour, like an oversized pack animal. My family files out and I follow my mother.

"Mom!"

She turns.

"Have a good trip," I say, hugging her.

She says thanks and I watch her get into the passenger seat of the car where she puts on her seat belt and rests her purse on her lap as she has done a million times before, except this time she does so with an air of childlike giddiness that is both cartoonish and endearing. I return to the house with a smile. She can't help it that her son is an asshole.

I find Wesley asleep on the couch with his mouth open. I carry him to his bed, his lips and fingers tinted orange from the Doritos he ate for dinner. I put cream on the impetigo around his nose and tuck him in.

Next door I find Joan in her room. She's taken all of the clothes out of her drawers. "Why did you do that?" She throws a shirt in the air. "Seriously, why did you take all of the clothes out of your dresser? Did you think that was a reasonable thing to do?"

"'Cause me hungry," she replies.

"That makes a lot of sense, Joan. Brilliant. I see the connection. Lie down. It's time for bed."

She kicks me a few times while I put on her diaper. Her fine ash hair sticks to her face with static. I blow it causing her eyes to blink. They are big eyes and dark as a meerkat's. I place her in her crib, say good night, and watch her flail from a crack in the door.

In the kitchen I pour a glass of red wine. Sometimes I miss smoking. As I pass through to the living room I consider what else I miss. It's a short list and includes getting laid and getting enough sleep and the blueberry cake my childhood neighbour made on special occasions. On the other hand, I don't miss Glen, the father of my children, his love for the Tragically Hip, the sleeveless shirts he wore to the gym, the crude size of his toenails. His early onset back fat and puffy

nipples. His penchant for forgetting people and reintrodu-
cing himself at social gatherings. He's always been this way.
Imperfect. And still I willingly procreated with him twice. At
the time the sex seemed rapturous and sublime. The kind of
rare and consummate experience when joy is carbonated and
cumbersome and completely engrossing, and you can't see the
keeper for the bees.

When I stretch out on the couch I notice it's mysteriously
damp. Joan has chewed off the power button on the remote
and I have to get up to turn on the TV. I switch it to A&E.
There is a man lying on the street under an overpass. It appears
he's been shot.

After the commercial break, detectives identify the victim.
He's only twenty. A father of two. They show pictures from
his prom in which he's wearing a dark suit and a gold vest. I
wonder if this is the same suit he wore at his funeral.

I fall asleep before finding out who killed Alphonse Jr.,
but I dream about him. It is one of those ordinary dreams
where I'm doing everyday things, except I have no pants on
and neither does Alphonse Jr. I wake up on the couch, disturbed. The lighter falls out of my pocket and onto the floor.

"Mommy!" Wes calls from his room. I ignore him, knowing he is likely still asleep, and stumble through the darkness
to my room across the hall.

It is 3:00 a.m. What the paranormal community refers to
as dead time. A period ironically said to be alive with super-
natural activity. Of Beetlejuice and Alphonse Jr. and my grandmother, as Rango, competing for atmospheric space or a closet
to inhabit or a crib-side seat to watch an infant sleep. But the
house is silent and after several adjustments of my pillow, I
am too.

The alarm goes off at 6:30 a.m. A reminder that today will be similar to yesterday and a lot like tomorrow. Routine. A short shower, no time to shave. Stale bread, toasted and the crusts removed. Instant oatmeal for Wes. Socks that don't match. No clean sippy cups.

"More milk!"

"How do you ask, Wes? Joan, come and eat your toast."

I unplug the toaster and plug in my hair dryer. I suggest Joan eat breakfast three more times before turning the dryer on high, but she is fixated on the TV listening to an overzealous yam puppet made from pantyhose — a yam with exaggerated lips that talks too loud and sings songs about lemonade with Ron Sexsmith. Most of the parents tuning into this morning's live performance of *Lemonade Stand* will not know him because he is not Bryan Adams or Celine Dion or the current face of Proactiv. I turn the TV off, and Joan reacts by slapping the screen.

"Eat your breakfast," I order.

"It garbage," she replies and promptly shoves it down her throat. I bend over and run my fingers furiously through my hair in an attempt to speed up the drying process. It gives me a head rush.

"Mommy!" Wes yells.

"What?" I holler back, glancing at him through my hair.

"What are you pointing at?"

"The thing!" he replies, waving his oat-soaked hand arbitrarily in my direction.

"What thing? The dishwasher? The toaster?"

"The hair dryer!" he yells.

I pull it away from the back of my head. It is smoking from both ends. I yank out the plug and the hair dryer makes a crackling noise reminiscent of Pop Rocks or knuckles. I try not to panic. To not imagine that it will set the house ablaze or electrocute me.

"Quick!" I say to Wes. "Go open the back door."

He slides off his chair with trepidation and runs to the back of the living room. "Is it going to explode?"

"No," I say, unconvinced, "but it's hot. Hurry up."

Indifferent to our terror, Joan turns the TV back on and sits down in front of it.

Wes flips the latch and tugs on the sliding door. It takes effort and I'm reminded of his smallness. He manages to open it a bit before it catches on the track above.

"Try again," I say.

"It's stuck!"

The hair dryer, that I am keeping as far away from my body as I can, slips in my grasp and the barrel singes my hand.

"Asshole."

Wes enjoys this and lets go of the door handle. He turns to face me and smiles. Maybe I'll kick the door or throw the hair dryer and tell it to fuck off.

"Move," I say, trying to squeeze through the narrow opening onto the deck, but I'm unsuccessful and resort, like Wes, to trying to open it further. Again it jams and I call it an asshole. Wes jumps up and down with perverse satisfaction. The yam on the TV starts crying because someone skipped breakfast or didn't recycle his juice box, and just before I launch into a feature presentation of rage, the sliding door falls clean off the tracks with the precision of a cliff diver.

I scream and catch the door with my shoulder, although I fumble my hold on the hair dryer — I snag its cord in my fist. As it dangles towards the floor I smell melted wires and failed mechanisms. I smell a plane crash. I lean the glass door against the wall so it won't fall over and step through the vacant space to the outside. I launch the hair dryer over the side of the deck.

Joan has joined her brother at the door, and watches curiously as I climb over the railing onto the grass.

"Wes, pass me the shovel!" I holler, pointing urgently at the shovel lying on the deck near the door.

He slides it through the rails to me.

I dig a hole, bury the hair dryer, and pat the earth down with my foot.

"Go put on your coats," I say, wiping my brow. "We're going to be late."

My children trip over each other, giggling and backing away from the door, and I swing the shovel up onto my shoulder in a chain gang sort of way and take the stairs up onto the deck.

There's now a hole leading into my living room. A leaf blows in like an intruder. I can't leave the house like this so I step inside the living room, strong-arm the door, slide it to the vacant space, and push it back into the track. It's not straight, but when I try a readjustment, it won't budge — no one's getting in, no one's getting out. When I step back and take a look at it, I realize it's like I'm securing my home as though it were a cave. But for today, it will have to do.

4

I drop the kids off at Turtle Grove Daycare. It is a squat stucco building with two wings, a boomerang of hurt feelings, pretend kitchens, and frizzy-haired teachers with varying degrees of back pain. Beside the front door there is a four-foot painted turtle with a speech bubble that says welcome friends, and though it wears a smile and has a Gay Pride shell, its anxious eyes are fixed on the roof.

After I kiss my children goodbye, Joan roams aimlessly searching for the meaning of it all, while Wesley runs to his friends at the back of the room.

"A door fell on my mom!" he says loudly.

I get back in the car and turn on the radio in search of a traffic report but find only morning shows discussing dating mishaps or playing music by people born in the nineties.

When I get to work, my assistant is using the large office kitchen sponge to clean up a coffee spill on her desk. The coffee is likely fair trade. She lifts up a framed picture of her sponsor child, wipes the desk underneath. Then she hands me a stack of phone messages that she took down for me, her writing bubble-like, juvenile, and in contrast to the steely unembellished Amnesty International postcards tacked up on her cubical walls. Phone numbers curl and swirl like they should be adorned with fairy dust or pink sugar. Letters are exaggerated as if each word carried an announcement of epic consequence: the birth of an heir to a throne, the eulogy of a pop star, two all-inclusive tickets to Cuba. In the case of the last message from the meat manager, top sirloin, *not* T-bone, is on special.

I grab this week's grocery flyer and confirm the error.

"Can you send out a correction notice?" I ask.

"Already done," she says, and shows me a picture of her newly painted kitchen on her iPhone. It's the green of unripe kiwi flesh. I consider my own kitchen, which is yellow like everyone else's, and has a border of roosters pecking at various heights. Several of them stare straight ahead as though posing for mug shots, their red combs crimped and bowed like beef jerky. But unlike most kitchen roosters with their stylized plumes and Tuscan shading, mine are photographs of real birds — the barnyard type who gang-rape hens and peck at small children.

I retreat to my office with the stack of messages and remain distracted by thoughts of my ugly house: the brass lighting fixtures, the dresser I've owned since childhood, the vertical drapes I have in common with my dentist's office. The blue carpet. Everything cheap and slightly gross like ranch dressing or a budding cold sore. I call Glen.

"Hey. You said you would take down the border in the kitchen and you never did."

"I'm about to go into a meeting. Is this important?"

"Yes, it's important. I still have a border in my kitchen."

"Right," he replies. "That is important. Would you like me to call 911?"

"You know what I mean."

"No actually, I don't. I have no idea why you thought it was necessary to call me while I'm working."

"Because you promised you would take it down and I'm tired of looking it."

"Well I didn't. I haven't got around to it yet."

"So you lied."

"Claudia, are you for real? I don't have time for this. If you are tired of looking at the border, then take it down yourself!"

I slam down the phone knocking a report off my desk and startling the intern walking by my office. He glances over then continues to his cube, his size fifteen feet pointing out at forty-five-degree angles like an enormous duck. I pick up the report and toss it on my filing cabinet and notice I have a voice mail. The message is from my mother.

She recites her flight information: "Air Canada Flight 643. It's a direct flight. Okay dear? We'll see you in a week. Kisses for Wes and Joan. Muahh!" She forgets to hang up. For several minutes she and my father discuss the whereabouts of his mouthwash. She assures him it's already packed and then tells him to put on his shoes.

"Not those ones," she says. "Those are your water shoes. I haven't cut the tags off yet."

"When did you buy them?" my father asks.

"First thing this morning at Walmart. I told you I was going out."

Then my dad asks who she's talking to, and my mother says oops and hangs up.

I call back to say goodbye, but no one picks up.

I take the next morning off work to get my hair done. It is too long, and the dark roots are exposed. The salon smells like toothpaste and a Christmas tree farm. The receptionist shows me to my chair and offers me a coffee.

"Hi, Claudia."

I spin around to see Allison-Jean lumbering through the salon towards the dryers. Her pregnant body resembles Grimace. Her hair is wet and tucked under a plastic cap.

"I didn't know you came here," I say, resting my coffee on my knee.

"It's my first time," she replies, sliding laboriously underneath a dryer with the assistance of her stylist.

"Your mom and dad seem to be having a nice time in Cuba," she says, turning her head slightly.

"You talked to them?" I move to the edge of my chair and closer to my sister-in-law.

"Last night. Your dad asked me to go by the house this morning to see if a package had arrived."

"What sort of package?" I speak loudly so she can hear me over the dryer's hum.

"He didn't say. Just something he ordered and forgot was coming today. He figured you and Daniel would both be at work." She winces from the heat of the dryer and shrinks down in her seat.

"What did you do to your hair?" I ask.

"Just a few highlights," she replies nervously. "I've never done anything with it before."

No kidding, I think. "Are you going to cut it too?"

"I haven't decided yet."

"You should cut it all off."

"No way!" she protests. "I could never do that."

"Why not?" I ask. "When was the last time you did anything crazy?"

Her stylist interrupts us to check on the progress of Allison-Jean's colour. She smiles with approval and pops the dryer back down.

"Well, are you cutting *your* hair?" she challenges.

"Yes," I reply.

"I don't know. I've never had short hair."

I place my coffee cup on the ledge below the mirror and adjust my cape. "So did you pick it up?" I ask.

"The package? No," she says, scratching her head, "it wasn't there."

"I can do it," I offer. "I have to go by there on my way home."

"Are you sure?"

"I'm sure."

She says thanks and attempts to sit more upright in her chair. I choose a magazine from a stack beside me and try to imagine what Allison-Jean would look like with short hair.

"The usual?" my stylist asks, examining my re-growth.

"Yep," I reply quietly so Allison-Jean can't hear.

She leaves to mix colour and I think of my parents tramping around their resort in matching water shoes — I suspect Dan said they were necessary for protection from a list of hazards he imagined, including hot sand, glass in the pool, and plantar warts.

I wonder if they will participate in any of the evening

entertainment: salsa lessons or comedy shows. Whether my mom will drink more than a glass of wine over the course of the entire week. Whether my dad will try his luck at wind-surfing or Ping-Pong. Briefly, I wonder if they will have sex there. Do they still have sex here?

In the opposite corner of the salon, Allison-Jean is walking to her chair, her hair now washed and wrapped in a towel. She chats with her stylist but I can't make out their conversation so I continue flipping through my magazine. By the time I am ushered over to the dryer to cook my own hair, Allison-Jean has lost most of hers. It lies at her feet in small dejected piles and she stares down at it in disbelief. I hide under the dryer and then watch as she feels the back of her head and inches closer to the mirror. One should not cut one's hair short while pregnant.

I leave the salon blond and guilty and head to my parents' house where there is indeed a FedEx package on the front steps. I take it back to the car and notice the front yard swing is broken. The plank I sat on as a kid hangs from a single piece of rope with the free end jammed into the muddy skid below. The other piece of rope hangs solo, frayed and blackened. I transfer the package to my hip and tug on the rope with my free hand.

I remember when Dan used to push me on the swing as hard as he could. He ate too many crescent rolls back then, and though he had the agility of a gibbon, pushing me left him breathless and sweaty. He always used a running start. I remember the whoosh of the air, the jerk of the swing at the top of the arc, the eavestrough beckoning the soles of my shoes as I swung towards the house, followed by the sudden plunge when one of the ropes came loose and the slap of the earth against the side of my body. Dan led me into the house where he administered first aid that consisted of patting my back, and looking at me with horror at his role in any injury I might have, but also awe at my bravery that if I was in pain, I wasn't showing it. Kind of like I just felt when Allison-Jean cut all her hair off.

I leave the dilapidated swing and get into my car.

At home I'm relieved to have some time to myself before I need to pick up the kids from daycare. The waybill on the top of Dad's package says TopStyler. I don't know what a TopStyler is so I take a knife and carefully slice open the box. Inside is a hair curling kit complete with an instructional DVD and styling wand. Why in the heck would Dad buy a hair curling kit?

I call Dan.

"Hey, did you know Dad asked Allison-Jean to pick up some package for him?"

"Yeah. Why?"

"Because I said I'd pick it up since I'm off today."

"Okay," he says blankly.

"It's a hair curling kit."

"You opened it?"

"Well it was sort of half-open."

"What do you mean by a hair curling kit? Like a curling iron?" Dan asks.

"No, like hot rollers."

"What for?"

"That's what I was going to ask you."

I turn on the kettle and go back to observe the TopStyler.

"He probably bought it for Mom."

"Mom doesn't use curlers. Besides, her hair is way too short for them."

"I don't know, Claudia." I hear him order a double double.

"Don't you think it's weird?"

"I don't know, maybe he bought them for someone else."
He honks at someone and yells, "Jackass!"

"Like who? Because I don't use curlers either." I pour hot
water into a mug and watch the tea bag inflate and float to
the surface.

"Maybe Allison-Jean can use them."

"Sure," I say. *Or not,* I think.

6

Later that night, Joan breaks crayons in half while Wesley plays with action figures in his bedroom. I can hear him interrogating them. "It was an accident," he says, "you acted in self-defense." His room is next to the living room and I realize he can probably hear what I watch at night. I wonder if he knows who killed Alphonse Jr.

When the kids are bathed and asleep, I make a plan to improve my kitchen. I grab a chisel from the toolbox and turn on the TV. I lower the volume and watch *Hoarders* with sick fascination because the people look normal but they collect things like newspapers or cats or school buses. Today's episode features a real estate agent. She wears a tailored cream suit, glossy pumps, and diamond cluster earrings. Pink and coral geraniums bend from the window boxes of her bungalow. She opens the front door and without removing her shoes swims to her bathroom like she's crowd surfing at a punk rock show. There's cat shit in her stand-up shower. Her sink is full of cosmetics and an open shoebox of photographs.

I stand on a chair in the corner of the kitchen and start scraping away at the roosters. Their eyes appear menacing in the low light and I cover them with my free hand as I scuff away at their ringed feet. I fetch a roll of duct tape from the junk drawer and proceed to tape over the eyes of all the forward-facing roosters. In a way they appear less offensive in their blindfolds. Or maybe they look tragic, victims of some barnyard atrocity. I find myself suddenly wanting to swaddle and pat them.

I climb off my chair for a break, lay the chisel on the table, and brush coiled bits of border from my clothes. The hoarder on *Hoarders* breaks down over the disposal of an ironing board. The phone rings.

"Hello?"

"Your mother's in the hospital," my father says faintly.

"With what?" I ask, thinking traveller's diarrhea. Hepatitis.

"A head injury," he replies.

"A head injury? How?"

A rat falls out of the hoarder's futon and runs frantically for cover.

"A banana boat."

"What do you mean?"

Furniture springs squeak. I assume he is now sitting. "She was *hit* by a banana boat."

"How do you mean, she was *hit* by a banana boat. What the hell's a banana boat?"

"It's a big yellow banana you sit on."

"Is it inflatable?"

"Yes. It's anchored down and towed by a boat."

He tells me my mother was swimming — I picture her, in her red bathing cap — and without the aid of her glasses mistakenly crossed the roped-in area to open water. Dad was straddling the fruit with a handful of other tourists. I picture them all ducking to avoid the spray of the sea as the boat slapped the waves. The banana jerking and fishtailing, drawing *oohs* and *ahhs* from its riders. Everyone blinded by sea salt and sun and unaware my mother had bobbed into the banana's erratic path. Then a thump, a soft yet definitive one, when the banana collided with my mother's head like a buoy and the *oohs* and *ahhs* ceased.

"How is she?" I ask.

He whispers, "I don't know."

"Come on, Dad, you said she was in the hospital. Is she speaking?"

My hands tremble and I feel sick and mighty with adrenaline. She-Ra. My father puts down the phone. The receiver smacks an unknown surface and he blows his nose.

"Dad?"

"No."

"No what?" I ask, agitated.

"She's not speaking."

"But she's okay?"

"They're looking after her. The doctors are very good."

I ask the same questions in slightly different ways hoping to extract more information about my mother's condition, but his answers remain the same. She is alive, she is okay, she is being looked after. We hang up with plans to talk tomorrow and I repeat my father's words: "She is alive, she is okay, she is being looked after."

I pace the kitchen, unsure of everything. Why am I here? Then I climb back up onto the chair with my chisel. A section of border peels clear with a single tug. I drop it to the floor and start scraping the next. It is less forgiving. Why was my mother swimming outside the roped-off area? Even without her glasses, didn't she have to duck under a rope? Why did no one notice her? I apply more pressure to the rooster. Why would the boat drive that close to the swimming area? Paper flutters to the floor. She doesn't even like swimming. She likes organized tours and museum talks. Not buffets and soca music. Maybe a driving range if she's feeling adventurous. She should be in Paris. I wipe my brow on my sleeve. I've cleared another three roosters along with much of the supporting drywall. The plaster dusts my countertops and cheeks like flour.

At breakfast Wesley looks up from his scrambled eggs and stares at the remains of the border in the kitchen.

"Why are some of the roosters wearing blindfolds?" he asks.

"They have cataracts. Like Grandpa."

He adds more ketchup to his egg while Joan counts her Mini-Wheats.

"One, sixteen, ninety hundred."

"What are cataracts?"

"It's when your eyes get cloudy."

"But Grandpa doesn't wear a blindfold."

"Yes, but Grandpa isn't a rooster. Finish your egg."

The phone rings.

"Who is it?" Wes asks.

"It's your Uncle Dan," I reply, looking at the call display.

"You heard about Mom?" my brother asks.

"Yes, Dad called last night."

"So, you haven't talked to him this morning?" He's upset.

"No," I reply, helping Joan down from her chair. "Get dressed," I whisper, pointing towards her room. "He called you this morning?"

"Mom is not doing so well," he says.

"What's different from last night?"

I jam diapers in Joan's backpack and glance up at the Turtle Grove Daycare calendar on the fridge.

"According to Dad, decreases in her motor and verbal responses."

The calendar indicates that today is Orange Day.

"Wes, go put on an orange shirt! Yesterday she wasn't even speaking. How can her verbal response *decrease*?"

"I don't know, Claudia. I just know that Dad said she was worse. I called and got a flight in a couple hours. I'm heading out now."

"Dad didn't call me." I toss Joan's backpack towards the front door. Wes hurries out of his room and parks himself an inch from the TV. "That is *not* an orange shirt, Wes. Go back and get an orange one. Dan, should *I* go?"

"It's up to you."

"I can't go!"

"No one said you had to," he says, irritated. "Geez."

"I can't just take off work like you."

He sighs. "Hold on a minute. It looks *fine*."

"What looks fine?"

He whispers, "Allison-Jean cut off all her hair."

"All of it?"

"Yes, all of it.

"And it looks fine?"

"No, it doesn't look fine, it looks horrible. Why would they do that to her?"

"I'm sure it looks fine."

"I promise!" he calls out from the mouthpiece. "You look beautiful."

"Just call me when you get there." I bite my tongue, then add, "Mom will be glad to see you."

I hang up the phone and search for orange clothes in my children's bedrooms and make Wes put on his soccer jersey.

"Do I have soccer today?"

"No."

"Then how come I'm wearing my soccer shirt?"

"Because it's Orange Day."

"And I have soccer on Orange Day?"

"No, Wes! You haven't had soccer in three months. Do you honestly think you were just randomly going to have soccer again?"

"Yes?"

I say *fuck* in my head and move on to Joan. I stop her from chewing her toenails and dress her in a peach shirt that is too small.

"We're going to be late," I tell them, gathering Wes's backpack, turning off the TV, and moving us all out the front door.

Outside the morning fog has yet to dissipate causing everything to appear under strain. A typical October day in Halifax: bare and wet, grey and swollen, the storm drains leaf-blocked and foaming, the pigeons distended and mumbling.

"Put on your seat belt, Wes."

I drop them off at Turtle Grove and return to the car wondering if the hospital in Cuba is white and institutional or resort-like and merrily inappropriate. I imagine the latter, a place saturated with colour and whimsy: fuchsia gauze and swan-shaped towels, umbrella-pricked cherries in the IV bags, and limbo competitions in the common room. When I leave the daycare I do not go to the office. Instead I call my boss and tell him about my mother, pledging to work from home as I wait for an update. He agrees and I leave Turtle Grove hopeful. The fog has lifted by the time I reach the house.

Glen is on the front step.

"What are you doing here?" I call out to him, retrieving my laptop from the passenger seat.

"I just ran into your brother at Starbucks. He said he was on his way to the airport. Your mom was in an accident?"

"Yeah, but she's okay," I assure him.

"Yeah?" He pauses. "Are you sure?"

"Yes, I'm sure. Dad said they were looking after her."

He paces around the front step while I fiddle with the key in the lock.

"Dan said she sounded pretty bad."

"Well yes, Glen, she got run over by a boat, but she is fine."

"Okay," Glen says defensively, "I just thought because Dan was going there that things were more serious than that."

I open the door and he follows me in. "He's mostly going to look out for my dad."

Glen rests his hands on his hips and exhales loudly. "That's good then."

"Besides, you know Dan. He overreacts to everything and needs to feel important. If anything he'll probably get in the way. Remember the time we went camping at Dollar Lake and it started storming and there was lightning? He told everyone to stand under a tree."

He shrugs. "Didn't you suggest we go in the tent?"

"A tent is safer than under a tree!"

"It was full of metal poles."

"Why are you still here?"

He sighs.

"If I needed to be in Cuba, my dad would have said, *Claudia, you need to come to Cuba*. Since when did you start wearing turtlenecks?"

"What's wrong with my turtleneck?"

"Nothing really."

"So you're fine then?"

"Yes, I'm fine."

"Tell your mom I'm thinking of her and that I hope she gets better quickly."

"Yep," I say, opening the door for him.

"Do you mind?" He hands me his empty Starbucks cup and heads out the door. I retreat to the kitchen and open my laptop and begin searching for flights to Cuba, placing Glen's coffee cup on the table beside me, wondering when he started drinking lattes.

I tell the kids about Grandma when I pick them up from Turtle Grove. Wes kicks at a pile of red and orange maple leafs.

"What happened?" he asks. "Did she eat too many Smarties?"

"No," I tell him, "she did not eat too many Smarties."

"Did she jump off a building?"

"Wesley! What kind of question is that? No, she didn't jump off a building. She was hit by a boat."

He says, "Cool."

"It's not cool," I tell him. "Grandma really hurt her head."

"Alexander's father got a nail in his eye and now he has a fake eye that he can pull in and out of his head. I think it's made of rubber." He pauses. "What kind of boat was it?"

I think before I respond. If I mention fruit, Wes will go to school tomorrow and tell his classmates Grandma was run over by a giant banana.

"A big one."

"Did she bleed?"

"It doesn't matter," I say, getting irritated. "She is very sick and we're going to go home and make her a get-well card."

I look at him in the rear-view mirror. I can tell he is dreaming up more gory details of his grandmother's fate. Joan picks at her blanket. She looks tired.

We get home and have breakfast for dinner. Afterwards I get an update from Dan, who's just visited Mom in the hospital.

"She looks like shit," he says. "Her face is purple and black and the sides of her head have been shaved. She's covered in stitches."

Joan's Cabbage Patch Kid pops into my head.

"Is she speaking?"

"Not yet. The doctors say that could be one of the side effects of a concussion."

"Concussion," I repeat. "But she's awake?"

"Yes, she's awake. She just doesn't respond when you talk to her."

"How's Dad?"

"He's a mess. He's still wearing his swim trunks."

"The red ones missing the crotch netting?"

"Yes, those ones."

"Well, frig, help him!"

"Claudia," he yells into the phone, "what the hell do you think I'm doing down here?"

"Put those dinosaurs back in the bin," I tell the kids, who pay no attention because *Chuggington* the asshole train is on.

"Is she allowed to fly home?"

"In a few days," Dan says, "but it might be a long recovery. Her arm is broken and her ribs are bruised." A calypso version of "I Just Called to Say I Love You" plays in the background.

"What's the hospital like?"

"It's okay," he says. "The beds are really small and there was quite a bit of dust underneath them, but the equipment looks modern and I saw the nurses washing their hands."

"Is she eating?"

"Seems to be. And I had her moved to a room with a window."

"I'm sure she appreciates that."

"Oh, she does."

I roll my eyes. "So it sounds like everything is under control."

"The doctor's optimistic."

"Good." I sigh. "I have software training."

"Oh," he says. Why am I telling him this? Our mother's in the hospital in Cuba.

"All day Friday. Saturday too." I qualify my busyness. "Hey, tell Mom I love her. And the kids are making her a card."

"Yep," he replies. "Okay, I need to go find Dad some pants."

I hang up and load the top rack of the dishwasher with glasses and watch milk drip through to the bottom. I think about my mother. Her broken arm and patched-up head. How she can knit sweaters and polish floors and roast things. How good she was in the delivery room when I had Wes, until she started singing. That part was annoying. I panic for a minute knowing I can't just hop in the car and go see her.

"Mommy?" Wes points a plastic gun the size of a toothpick at my face.

"Yes?"

"Why are you putting dirty dishes in the dishwasher?"

"Because they're dirty, Wes, and don't point that thing at my face."

"Those ones aren't," he says, pointing at dishes in the bottom rack.

I take the gun and toss it on the counter. "Well, they are now."

"Is Grandma going to die?"

"Of course not." I ruffle his brown hair.

"Are you sure?"

"Yes, I'm sure."

"So she's still going to bring me something back from her trip?"

I close the dishwasher and lean against it with my arms crossed. My look is one of disappointment but it goes over

Wesley's head. He retrieves the gun and spins it in his hands, waiting for my response.

"Your question is inappropriate."

He rolls his eyes and leaves the room. Stops momentarily to discard his socks. His feet are delicate and narrow and I remember kissing them in the delivery room when he was new and pristine and tasted like heaven.

"Brush your teeth," I call after him.

I get a second wind when they're in bed, pour a glass of wine, and paint my toenails a garish pink in the living room. Napa Valley wine, brothel-like polish. I stare at the wall between coats and try to imagine my mother's face, but all I see is the French woman who had the first face transplant. Her chin is small and pointy. Nothing like my mother's, which is wide and rather square. I reach for my lip balm in the dimly lit room. I have her thin lips.

Dan sends a text in the morning. Mom is acting strange. She can't taste her food and her blood pressure has dropped.

I text back, *What does the doctor think?*

He writes, *He says all her symptoms are typical of a head injury.*

I reply, *Let me know if anything changes.*

I get ready for work.

After dropping the kids off at Turtle Grove, I call Glen and ask him if he can take the kids to daycare tomorrow morning and pick them up after, for his weekend with the kids. It's a bit of a special request, but he's always liked my mother. She indulged him. Praised his accomplishments, stocked relish in her fridge for him. He agrees to the extra day of parenting.

At work I am hustled into meetings for most of the morning. I periodically check my phone for updates.

Dan sends me a picture of a skinny cat with a tight ball-sack outside their suite at the resort with the message: *mom in physio this morning.*

I reply, *is she being neutered?*

He ignores my joke and sends the correct thumbnail of my mother. She appears to be performing circles with her good arm. The other is tucked beneath her nightgown. The side of her head is shaved as Dan described.

She doesn't look too bad, I write.

Look at her face, he replies.

I zoom in on my mother's head and observe the network of stitches on her cheek. Her eye is black. The nurse in the background wears a white cap on her head and is standing in front of a barred window.

Does that window have bars on it?

My brother doesn't reply.

The kids come home from daycare with collages of orange things.

"What's that?" I ask Joan, pointing to a series of lines on her picture.

"Dat's a cat squirrel," she replies.

"What's a cat squirrel?"

"It orange."

"Oh. Thanks for clarifying that." I stick her picture on the fridge on top of some others, but the magnet fails and a pile of artwork sails to the floor. She helps pick it up.

"I'll put the cat squirrel on top," I say, filing through the stack.

"Put mine up too!" Wes chimes in, presenting his own collage. "That's you Mommy," he says, pointing to a person in an orange T-shirt with what appears to be a cleft palate.

"Nice, Wes. Listen kids, Daddy is going to pick you up tomorrow morning."

"Why?"

"Because Mommy has to work tomorrow and I have to be there really early."

"Can me come?" Joan asks.

I correct her, "Can *I* come. And no."

"I thought we were going to make Grandma a get-well card?"

"Yes, but I think instead of a card we'll make her a welcome-home sign we can take to the airport."

Wes jumps with enthusiasm. I tell him to get the craft box from the shelf. Then I hear a familiar knuckle knock on the door — the one where Glen doesn't wait for me to open it

"What's up?" I say.

He wipes his feet in the entry and takes off his jacket, which is wet. "My last appointment cancelled," he says, shivering. "Thought I'd take them tonight. Give you some extra time in the morning."

"Right." I ask him, "Are you still selling speculums?"

"No," he says. "Neurological products."

I stare at him.

"Genetic tests. To detect things like epilepsy."

"What else?"

"Alzheimer's, Huntington's disease, some cancers." He fixes his hair in the mirror. "I told you that a while ago."

This is when he started drinking lattes. Tim Horton's was fine when he sold what Wes referred to as "water guns to open your front bum."

"We haven't even eaten dinner."

"What are you making?" Glen asks Wes, moving past me and kissing him on the cheek.

"A welcome-back sign for Grandma."

"Wes," I interject, "you need a bigger piece of paper. Grandma will not be able to read that."

He sighs and moves the apple-shaped Post-it note to the side, and then he grabs the jumbo pad of construction paper from Joan's hands. She stands up in her chair and screams before jabbing him in the forehead with a marker. Glen and I each grab a kid before the situation escalates.

"I'm hungry," Wes cries.

I tell him to choose a piece of paper from the pad and then give it back to Joan while I search the cupboards for something to eat. Our options are canned salmon, slivered almonds, and Panko breadcrumbs.

"Why don't I buy pizza?" Glen offers.

"You're staying for dinner?" I hike up my jeans, which are loose from not being washed.

"Not if you're having that," he says, pointing to the salmon.

"Fine. Order pizza. And don't get pineapple on it because you're the only one who likes it."

"Wes likes pineapple on his pizza."

"No, he doesn't."

"Yes, he does."

"Wesley, do you like pineapple on your pizza?"

He looks up from the construction paper and nods absent-mindedly.

"Take the wrestler out of your mouth," I order. "You're going to hurt your teeth."

He removes it for a second, but soon goes back to chewing the figurine's head while he flips pages.

"So pineapple on half then."

Glen goes into the living room to order the pizza. Wes begins to whine.

"Stop whining, Wes."

"But all the pages are marked."

"There are four hundred pages in that book. They can't all be marked."

"But they are," he says, crying.

"Give it to me." I snatch the book from him and begin flipping through the pages. They are all marked.

"Fuck," I mumble under my breath.

"See?" Wes says, spinning around in his chair.

"Joan you can't make a scribble on every page," I say, holding up the book.

"Cat squirrel," she responds.

"Do you want ham or pepperoni?" Glen hollers from the living room, covering the mouthpiece of the receiver.

"Ham!" I yell, tearing the least scribbled page out of the book. "Just use the other side."

Wes takes the paper reluctantly and asks me to spell "welcome home." I pick up one of the few markers that still has its top, and write in block letters for him to colour in. The marker quits before I finish, so the Home is fainter than the Welcome.

"Start on that," I say. He obliges, filling in the letters with an assortment of colours. I clean up the breakfast dishes while Glen and Joan watch TV.

"I'm going to get their stuff ready."

Glen nods and smiles.

"What?" I ask.

"Nothing," he says.

I turn down the hall and begin packing their bags with pajamas and school clothes. I find a banana in Joan's sock drawer at the same time my phone plays the xylophone indicating I have a message.

Dan's text says, *mom will be discharged on Friday or Saturday.*

Thank God, I reply, sinking into Wes's bed.

Coming home Sunday, he adds.

I write, *see you then,* and lie flat on the bed. I remember when Wes used to force both Glen and me to lie with him. The discomfort. Our attempts to creep out without him waking up. The doorbell rings.

"Grandma!" Wes yells. I hear his chair push back from the table.

"I'll get it," Glen says. "It's probably the pizza." He steps loud and heavy towards the front door.

"Why do you walk like that?" I say, although he's not in earshot. I get up and watch Wes scramble in front of Glen, with his sign.

"Grandma is in Cuba," I remind Wes, but he holds up the sign anyway as Glen opens the door.

"Hi," Wes says.

The delivery driver ignores Wes and hands the pizza to Glen.

"Come away from the door, Wes," I say, tugging at his shirt.

I take the pizza from Glen and head to the kitchen. Wes follows and hangs off me.

"Get off my arm!" I yell, placing the box on the table. "You almost made me drop it."

He sits on top of the table and says, "I want six pieces."

Glen joins us in the kitchen. He removes Wes from the table and places him in a chair.

"Where's Joan?" I ask, looking at Glen and Wes.

They both shrug and simultaneously take slices of pizza using their hands as plates. I sigh. Joan arrives at the table and kneels on her chair. One fist is clenched.

"What do you have there?" I ask.

She opens her hand and reveals a pile of her hair.

"Nice, Joan. Perfect."

Mom's released from the hospital on Friday. They want to keep her close by for a couple days, but she's back on the resort with my father and brother. Dan sends pictures. My mother appears sunburned but mobile and surprisingly content. I tell Dan the kids and I will meet them at the airport Sunday, and he says that's fine.

I spend the next two days in and out of training. Our software is being upgraded. What could have been taught in two hours is spread out over two days. I spend some of the time proofing a series of new banners that will hang in our produce departments. Pictures of giant artichokes and dewy peaches paired with their respective growers.

I spend my last childfree hours Sunday afternoon working on the kitchen and invite my friend Cathy to help. She is resourceful, single, and a heavy-duty mechanic. She runs her own shop. I have known her since elementary school and though she is over six feet tall, a veritable Viking, she has a feminine face and hair she can pin-curl. A bombshell on stilts without a lick of athletic talent. She enters without knocking.

"Hello, hello," she says, holding a tray of Starbucks. "They didn't have any peppermint so I got you chamomile instead."

"You are awesome," I say, taking the drinks to the kitchen.

She removes her leather jacket and hangs it on the back of a chair, nearly tipping it over. "You're getting rid of the roosters," she observes.

"Finally," I reply, passing her the chisel.

I take the lid off my cup and remove the teabag. Cathy ascends the stepstool, her head bent to the side, and begins scratching away at one of the birds.

"When do the kids get back?"

"Around six. Glen will have fed them because we're meeting my parents at the airport."

"Did they finally go to Paris?"

"No," I reply, slurping my tea. "They went to Cuba."

"Cuba?"

"Yeah, my brother paid for it."

"Go Dan," she replies, moving the stepstool to the next rooster.

"Except my mom got hit by a boat and had to go to the hospital."

Cathy stops chiselling. "But she's okay?"

"Yes, thank God. I think it was just a mild concussion."

"What a sin." She exhales with relief and descends the stepstool. She picks up her tea, takes a sip, pushes her hip to the side. I stare at her curiously. "I just came from the chiro," she explains. "My hip was out."

"Weren't you there yesterday too?"

"That was for my back."

"So how often do you go to the chiropractor?"

"Two to three times a week. Depending."

I barely shower three times a week. "Wow."

"You should do it," she says. "Even just to get assessed."

"My back is good."

Cathy shrugs. She looks out into the living room. "What's with your door?"

"It's a long story," I reply.

She goes to the back door. "Is it even on the track?"

"It's *in* the track. My dad said he fixed it. And then we tried to go outside and it attacked us."

"Your father was never a handyman. Remember the time he tried to fix your bike?"

"Yes," I groan.

"Didn't he put the seat on backwards or something?"

"The handlebars."

"Right." She laughs. "And you could never drive in a straight line afterwards. I remember that bike. It was too big for you."

"That's because it was my brother's. He never rode it."

Cathy removes the door effortlessly, props it against her knee, and properly places it on the track. She bends over the toolbox that's still in the living room, where my dad left it. She pulls out a screwdriver.

"How is your brother anyway?" Cathy asks. "Did they have their baby?"

"No, she's due sometime before Christmas. He's fine."

Cathy uses her shirt to buff out a handprint on the glass.

"He's actually on his way back from Cuba with my parents. He flew out there when my mom got hurt to play rescue hero."

In response, Cathy does a ninja kick.

"Wow. That looked surprisingly natural."

She shrugs. "Must be the parkour."

"The what?"

"Parkour. It's like track and field but downtown. You jump over benches and stuff. Climb walls. It builds coordination and agility." She pushes a curl away from her face.

I am bewildered. "Who signs up for this stuff? I mean, who else besides you?"

"All sorts of people. Watch." She slides open the door —

demonstrating that she has indeed fixed it — takes two giant steps back, then runs outside and vaults over the deck railing to the grass below. "That's parkour!" she yells from the lawn.

Parkour is disturbing. Like nightclub dancing or naked maid service.

Cathy hops up onto the deck. She looks pleased and is slightly out of breath.

"Nice," I say. "Where in the heck did you discover parkour?"

"In the community recreation guide."

We return to the kitchen and finish our tea. Mine is lukewarm.

"Thanks for fixing the door."

After Cathy leaves I take off my bra, microwave leftover lasagna, and eat it standing. The top noodles are overcooked and hard. There are still bits of wallpaper on the floor. I corral them into the corner with my sock and put away the toolbox. Dan sends a text to say their flight is delayed an hour. I sigh, knowing it will be too late to meet them now. The kids will be home soon and disappointed.

I quickly search Joan's room for the *I Spy* book I hate so I can hide it. Forty pages of creepy collages: masquerade masks, red lipstick, vintage clowns, antique dolls. It's like a scrapbook from the set of *Saw*. *I spy with my little eye a lampshade made of skin.* I find it just as Glen arrives.

"Hello," he calls, Joan pushing in front of him.

I drop her book in the oven drawer and kick it shut.

"Mama," she says, pulling off her socks. I kiss her on the cheek and taste ketchup.

"Where's Wes?" I ask Glen.

"Coming," he replies. "He forgot something in the car."

Wes appears minutes later with a Transformers figure.

"I gotta run," he says, dropping the kids' bags in the hall.

"Okay," I say, picking up Joan's socks. "Thanks for taking them."

"Yeah, no problem." He calls for Joan and Wes to come say goodbye then jogs down the front steps to his car.

"How was your weekend, bud?"

"I'm starving."

"You're starving? Didn't Daddy just feed you?"

"Yeah, but it was disgusting. He made us eat long things."

I make him toast and peanut butter and wonder about the long things before searching for Joan. I find her curled up at the end of her bed nearly asleep.

"Did Joan eat her long things?" I ask Wes, returning to the kitchen.

He nods, wipes peanut butter from his cheek. I get Joan's blanket from the front hall and tuck her in properly. Wes appears at her door holding the Welcome Ho sign.

"We never finished the sign!" he says, alarmed.

"I know," I say, hushing him with my finger. "We can finish it tomorrow."

"But Dad said the airport was tonight."

I guide him out of Joan's room and explain, "Their flight is delayed."

"But I want to go to the airport."

"Another time," I assure him, putting the sign on the top of the fridge. He is too tired to argue. I motion for him to climb onto my back and carry him to the couch. He pulls a blanket over his lower half.

"Did you have fun at Daddy's?" I ask, pulling him close.

"Yeah," he replies. "Can you get my Optimus Prime?"

I look towards the front hall and muster the energy to get up. I move Wes off of me and go to the kitchen. Optimus Prime is on the table. It is neither vehicle nor robot but somewhere in between. A pupa of plastic made in China. One leg, half a front bumper, a single headlight. I fiddle with it, attempt to convert it into a car, but can't figure out how to get the wheels out so I instead try to make it a robot. I fail. It now has a wheel, two arms, and a head. Asshole.

"Who bought this for you?" I ask from the kitchen.

Wes pokes up from behind the arm of the couch. "Daddy."

"Well it doesn't work."

He slides off the couch and retrieves it anxiously. He pushes the robot's head and swivels its limbs until it looks like an ambulance.

"See?" he says, showing it off. "It works." He returns to the couch and gets back under the blanket.

"Bedtime," I say, scooping him up, carrying him to his room, and placing him in his bed. "Love you, Wes."

I return to the kitchen, pour a glass of wine, and examine the ambulance. I find the robot's legs tucked in the back. Sirens and a steering wheel but no place for a stretcher. I release them. It is now a vehicular Centaur. I flick it towards the sugar bowl.

After nine the phone rings. It's Dan. He tells me that somewhere over Sable Island on Air Canada Flight 919, my mother passed away of a massive stroke.

Initially I can't comprehend the news. I say okay as though he's told me to take out the garbage, and I hang up the phone. I stumble to the table and knock over my glass, which hits the sugar bowl with an audible clink. The kind of sound that should precede a kiss or follow a toast. I think of the island. Its impossible thinness. An eyelash in the sea. Its wild horses, silver-haired bats, and the seals. The seals! Dragged to the bottom of the ocean by Greenland sharks, blind and obtuse and out of nowhere. I think of their descent into the dark. The sudden quiet. Mom flipping through a magazine or righting her blouse or buttering my father's bread when the blood began to clot and parts of her brain started to die off. Little bits of Janice disappearing like the contents of an advent calendar. Memories and facts snuffed out, cell by cell. Her brain, like the island, made virtually invisible by the darkness of night. Porch lights extinguished, lighthouse dead in the fog. My mother in the aisle, flanked by the plane's emergency lights, with the seals below and my father above and the ponies roaming aimlessly between. The phone rings again.

"You hung up," Dan says.

I try to stand but lose my footing and fall to my knees. Wes's Transformer lies face down in the puddle of wine on the table.

"I know," I reply.

"She's gone," he says, and it sounds less permanent this way. Like she might be gone to get milk or an oil change.

"I know."

"And she's not coming back." He breaks down and sobs. Noises tumble out of his mouth like vomit. Breath all chopped up, chest in a blender.

"Where are you?" I ask. My house is so quiet.

"Yarmouth," he whispers.

"Where's Mom?"

"Hospital," he says, passing off the phone. The exchange is messy.

I wait for my dad.

"Dad?" I ask. "Are you there, Dad?"

"Claudia . . . she just . . . she was just going to stretch her legs."

I wipe my eyes with the heels of my hands.

"They put her in the basement. She's in the basement over there. They shouldn't put them in the basement. Basements are cold. She doesn't have her slippers."

I take the phone away from my ear and sob like my brother. Dan whispers from my lap they will call tomorrow. I hang up and toss the phone on the counter. It spins and comes to a stop beside the knife block.

"Are you looking for something, Mommy?" Wes wanders down the hall towards the kitchen.

"Your Transformer," I say.

"It's on the table," he says. "Beside you."

"Right," I reply, pulling myself up. I pick up Optimus Prime.

"Yuck," Wes says. "Why is he all wet? He smells like the place we take the recycling to."

"He went swimming," I explain.

I towel-dry the transformer and carry Wes back to bed.

"You okay, Mommy?"

I nod and pull the covers up to his chin. He has Glen's chin, pointed with a slight depression. I stroke it with my fingertip.

"Will you sing?"

"Sing what?" I ask.

"Anything."

I can't think of anything to sing. I try to remember what my mom sang to me but I can only think of Rita MacNeil and the Men of the Deeps and the jingle from Sleep Country that makes me want to knife my mattress. My mother could not sing. She had no range and made up lyrics. Replaced entire phrases with humming. Wes waits for it to begin. I take a deep breath and make up a song about the transformer.

"You used to be an ambulance . . ."

Wes is unsure about this song. He turns onto his side and closes his eyes. I back out of the room, making up lyrics, inventing a chorus that has Optimus Prime wishing for his legs. I feel heady and nauseous and slump back down at the kitchen table, which is still sticky from the wine. Mom needs her slippers. I can go to her house and get them and drive them to her. Yarmouth is only three hours away. Four hours? Three and a half? How do I get to Yarmouth? Is it the 102 or the 103? I will put the kids in the car and drive south and bring Mom her slippers. I slide on my Toms, look in the fridge for my keys. A cantaloupe rolls out, which I kick. *Fuck you.* I go to my laptop and google hospitals in Yarmouth. *Yarmouth Regional. Providing care to 64,000 people in Shelburne, Yarmouth, and Digby Counties.* Care? Is that what they call it? Putting mommies in the basement without their slippers? Maybe I could take her a sleeping bag. There should be one in the linen closet. A double one from when Glen and I went camping. I tear the closet apart until I'm surrounded by a heap of towels, most of them pilled, all of them old. And piles of sheets. Fitted ones all bunched up like beehives. Pillowcases I never iron. On my tiptoes I pull on the top shelf, straining to see, it creaks with my weight. There's the sleeping bag in the back, and I yank it by the cord of its polyester sheath. It tumbles on top of me, like a fabric sausage. I pull until it's completely free from its shell: navy plaid, unwashed, smelling like wood smoke. I climb inside.

I wear sunglasses at breakfast. We eat Corn Flakes. I don't tell them about Grandma. I find a note from Turtle Grove in Joan's backpack saying she needs more diapers. I search the house and manage to scrounge up four. It is an ordinary day. On the way to daycare we pass the same woman walking to work that we always do. Her gait and headband are the same. We get the red light by the high school. Wesley talks the entire way. Of zombies and Japan and the corn twists he never gets in his lunch. I want to tell him to shut up. I want to scream it.

I park by the door and walk them inside. The daycare director approaches.

"How's your mom?" she says in a voice that's just above a whisper.

I shake my head. She covers her mouth.

"I'm sorry," she says touching my arm.

"I haven't told the kids yet."

"If you need anything, please don't hesitate —"

"I could only find four diapers," I interrupt.

She waves me off and says, "Don't worry about the diapers."

I call work from the car and share the news. Stroke on a plane. No slippers in the morgue.

Then I drive by my parents' house where the swing is still broken and the trees have lost all their leaves. The house looks different this morning. Locked up and less an owner. Quiet and weary after decades of dirty hands and grass clippings and

Christmas lights. A package juts out of the mailbox. I park and walk up the driveway, stepping over the cracks in the asphalt as I have since childhood, and I pick up the mail. Along with a package addressed to my father is a coupon for ten percent off furnace cleaning. Will she be cremated? I toss both the flyer and the package in the front passenger seat and drive home.

When *The View* comes on, I cry because Elisabeth's a Republican and Barbara pretends she's not an octogenarian. She thinks she's fifty like a dog thinks it's human. When Glen calls, I explain this to him, between spoonfuls of my second bowl of Corn Flakes.

"Why are you home?" he asks.

"My mother died last night. On the plane."

"On the plane?"

"They were coming home from Cuba."

"I thought you said she was okay?"

"She was okay! She had a stroke."

"Because she hit her head?"

"I don't know Glen, I'm not a friggin' doctor. I just know she had a stroke. On the plane. Were you calling for something specific?"

"No, I was just going to leave a message. I think I left my sunglasses there. I'm coming over."

We hang up and I yell at Barbara, "You're fucking eighty!"

Glen shows up with apple turnovers from Costco and Kleenex with the built-in lotion.

"I brought you some ginger ale," he says, twisting off the cap.

"I'm not sick, Glen."

"I know but I didn't know what else to get."

He hands me the bottle and parks himself on the coffee table. "I'm sorry, Claud."

He paces around the room when my father calls. Dad's thoughts are all over the place.

"Your mom loved carnations. The price of gas went up overnight. Dan has never eaten a hard-boiled egg."

I respond with like comments: "Joan wants to be a cat squirrel for Halloween. I think Mom would want a white casket. One of those glossy ones like the cabinets you see in the show homes. There are forty grams of fat in a carrot muffin."

Glen gives me an odd look and turns off *The View*. Dad asks what a cat squirrel is and explains that Mom wanted Stompin' Tom Connors played at her funeral.

"What song?" I am only able to recall the Hockey Song and the PEI tourism jingle. Dad does not reply. I hear him ask Dan where his glasses are. Glen holds up a turnover. I nod and he puts one on a plate.

"Thanks," I tell him.

"What was that, dear?" Dad asks.

"Nothing. Listen, how are you getting home?"

"Your brother's renting a car."

"Are you sure Dan should be driving? I mean . . . this soon?"

"We're not leaving until tomorrow. We have to make arrangements to have your mother moved first."

"Call me before you leave. Okay? I love you, Dad."

I pick at the turnover.

"How is he?" Glen asks, taking a second turnover from the plastic tray.

"I don't think he's slept."

Minutes go by. I stare at the ceiling and start humming the Hockey Song. All I know is the chorus. After a few times Glen begins whistling along.

"She wants Stompin' Tom played at her funeral."

Glen collects LEGO from the carpet. "That's right," Glen says, waving his finger. "I remember her telling me that once."

"My mom discussed her funeral with you?"

"No, no. Just that she liked him. What song are you going to play?"

"No idea. Dad didn't know. What other songs are there?"

"'The Sasquatch Song,' 'The Snowmobile Song,' 'Margo's Cargo'. . ."

I glare at him.

"What?" he says defensively. "I don't know. Go look them up."

I take my laptop out of the bag along with a pink cup and saucer and a fake egg. It is a habit of Joan's to stow away parts of her tea set so in the event of a natural disaster we can still have a tea party. I google Stompin' Tom and get a website with his discography. There are hundreds of songs. I scroll down the track lists for something appropriately titled for a funeral.

"Ever hear of 'I Am the Wind?'"

"How does it go?" Glen asks from the bathroom.

"I don't know."

"What else is there?"

"'Just a Blue Moon Away'?"

"Nope. Never heard of it.

I keep scrolling and find one called "Rubberhead" and I start laughing because of the irony and it's absolutely not funny, and because of this I laugh more. My stomach throbs and I cover my face with an afghan. It smells like yogurt, but I keep my face under there because I am completely ashamed and still laughing. When I come up for air, Glen's emerging from the bathroom and it looks like he has toothpaste on his chin and I am suspicious he's used my toothbrush.

He touches my shoulder and says, "It's going to be okay." I pull the afghan away. The smell is unbearable and I've gained control and I wipe at my eyes, but when I think about the song I start laughing again.

"Are you . . . *laughing?*" Glen says, walking around to the front of the couch.

I shake my head. I fall into the arm of the couch and the laughter turns into crying because only evil people would find "Rubberhead" amusing under the circumstances. Glen takes the laptop and sets it on the coffee table. He pulls me by the arm up to a sitting position, continues scrolling down the screen, and there, second-last track from the bottom, he finds "Sable Island."

"That will work," I say.

After supper I take the kids to Dairy Queen. They both order Dilly Bars. I choke down a cheeseburger in three bites. We sit in the parking lot across from a couple in a car with two doors, who smoke out their windows, flicking ashes into the wind. Our car smells like pickles. I turn off the engine and tell the kids about their grandmother. The chocolate around Joan's mouth looks like facial hair, but my attempts to clean it off are futile from the front seat.

"How'd she die?" Wesley asks. His eyebrows furl like his father's when he is contemplating something.

"She had something called a stroke."

"Because she got hit by the boat?"

"Sort of," I say, still unsure whether the events are connected.

"Where is she?"

"She's in heaven," I explain.

Joan asks, "With Jesus?"

"Yes, with Jesus," I reply, turning in my seat to face her. It hurts my neck.

"Who else is there?" Wesley wants to know.

"Lots of people, I suppose."

"He like Dilly Bars?"

"Does who like Dilly Bars, Joan?"

"Jesus."

I remove a peanut from my sundae and crunch into it. "I'm sure Jesus likes Dilly Bars."

Joan breaks her Dilly Bar stick in half.

"Is Grandpa going to go to heaven too?" Wes asks.

"Someday."

"But they go everywhere together." He leans his head against the window and points to an inflatable pumpkin on top of a car dealership. "We don't have a pumpkin," he says. His eyes fill with tears.

"You're right." Halloween is tomorrow or next week. Is it today? "Let's go get one right now."

We drive across the parking lot to the grocery store. I check my iPhone. Right, it's the 24th of October. Mom has only been dead for one day. The kids have no costumes, but we don't need to panic about a pumpkin quite yet.

"What do you want to be for Halloween?" I ask Wes, unbuckling him from his car seat.

"I want to be . . ." he pauses and places his finger on his chin. "A pirate!"

"What about me?" Joan chimes.

"You already told me you wanted to be a cat squirrel."

"No," she argues.

"Well what then?"

"Me want to be a stroke."

By the next day, I'm carving pumpkins and cutting costume pieces out of discount fabrics. The kitchen table is taken over by seeds and pipe cleaners and scraps of felt. I'm constantly moving needles and sharp things to the centre of the table where Joan is less likely to get at them. Scattered in between our decorations are notes on the funeral. Times and dates and estimates on everything from catering to caskets. There are lists of psalms and sheet music. "Sable Island" does not make the cut.

Dan calls. "What if we framed some of her favourite recipes and displayed them at the visitation Friday?"

"What?"

"They were sort of her claim to fame."

"Yeah, but you don't do that."

"Why not? I think she'd like it."

"No." I take a sewing needle from the wine glass and scrape my teeth.

"Her pecan and goat cheese salad, beef stroganoff, and blueberry grunt. I already had Allison-Jean print them off on cardstock."

"That's great, Dan. Is she printing off a wine list too?"

"And what if we had one of her former students give a eulogy?"

"The funeral's in four days."

"It would be just a few words about Mom as a teacher."

"She taught grade two." I poke my gums until they start to bleed.

"So? They'd be grown-up now. It could be nice."

"Are you nuts? Have you ever been to a funeral?"

"I'm just trying to make it special!"

"A recipe for blueberry crisp and some former student's memory of how she taught them to spell 'cat' does not make it special."

"Blueberry grunt."

"No!"

"You're being difficult."

"You're being ridiculous!"

He sniffs into the phone like he might be crying. I sigh. "You should be the one doing the eulogy. I'll pick her dress and make sure her makeup looks okay. All she'd really care about is that no one fights and she's wearing pantyhose. Okay?"

"And the recipes."

"If it's that important to you, display the recipes. And," *fuck*, "do you think Allison-Jean could make Joan a cat squirrel costume?"

"A what?"

I give the phone to Joan to tell Allison-Jean what a cat squirrel is.

After the kids are both in bed, I pour a glass of wine and start one of the tasks I've been putting off: sorting through photos. I dump out a Ziploc bag marked vacation.

They're not vacation photos, though. They date back to when we were in junior high. When I had a perm and Dan still had a weight problem. In one of them he has a black eye. Darrell Wilson kicked the shit out of him because Dan was fat and was in his way. Darrell Wilson who smoked rolled cigarettes and wore jean jackets and had sex with Miranda

Coughlin, who worked at Tim Horton's, when he was twelve. Sex with someone who had a job! Darrell Wilson with his cauliflower ear who was probably abused and didn't have his sheets cleaned regularly and ate dinner at a card table. Dan staggering, blubbering, bruising, white flesh hanging. His textbooks scattered over the parking lot. And I hollered after Darrell Wilson, "You have a grandpa for a Dad!" Dan lost weight after that.

There's another bag, helpfully Sharpied Photos. It's full of pictures of my parents, and it is as Wesley said: they went everywhere together. My mother, wearing the same white sneakers over a ten-year period, with my father, his arm around her shoulders, their hips touching, but just barely. She wears walking shorts and sleeveless blouses. On the boardwalk, in a city, on a trip I don't remember them taking. On the ferry to PEI and perched on the picnic table in Dan's backyard. The pictures from winter are older. She is thinner and wears a full-length coat with a fur collar. Same pose, but Dad carries a snowball in his hand and his cowlick looks more severe. Always together. What will he do without her?

On October 28th, a cool day, an old baseball friend of Dad's drives us to the funeral home for the visitation. I sit sideways behind him to avoid his reclined seat and stare at his elbow, which is bare and crusty and resembles the breading my mom used to put on halibut. Strips of toilet paper hang from the birch tree outside of the funeral home. Kids are getting a head start on their Halloween shenanigans. The director, dressed in grey pinstripes, tries to pull them down, but they blow out of reach, almost playfully.

"I'll have them removed at once," he says as we exit the car. He mumbles something about kids, shakes my father's hand, and shows us inside. Allison-Jean does not wear one of her signature peasant shirts today because she will be playing the piano during the visitation. Instead she wears a long floral dress and Tabi cardigan. She sets her purse on the bench as the rest of us tour the two rooms where things will take place. My mother has a cherry-coloured casket that matches the funeral home's piano. It is closed and covered with large pink and red carnations. Is she on her side the way she slept? My father chose ivory satin for the interior to match her pearls. Beside the guest book, her recipes stand in frames.

Dan takes over discussions with the funeral director and makes small adjustments to the setup. He turns framed photos millimetres to the left or right and tugs on one of the home's navy velvet curtains so it is drawn the same distance as its companion. Dad and his friend Bill stand by the window, and Bill pats Dad on the back. My father looks down and traces the diamond pattern in the carpet with his shoe, which is not polished and looks dull against the glow of the casket. In the other room, Allison begins playing the piano. A few notes at first. A scale, followed by another, then she plays something I've heard my mother hum before but I don't know its name.

People will start pouring in over the next half-hour. I think of the kids at Turtle Grove Daycare. Snack time is almost under way. I wonder if Joan has tried to hit anyone today and what games Wesley is forcing on his friends. The piano stops but I can hear Dad continue to hum, from across the room — that's what it's called, "Just As I Am."

"People are coming," Dan says, centering his belt. His hair is freshly cut.

I wait for them. Just as I am. Legs unshaven, skin tag on the back of my neck. New underwear, no mascara. I watch Dan trip as he walks to the other room. He meets Allison-Jean halfway. Their embrace is awkward on account of her pregnant belly, which looks considerably bigger since my mother's birthday. They love each other. Despite bad haircuts and large pores and window valences covered with cats. His kid-size feet. Her collection of Precious Moments figurines. Just as they are, and it makes me feel alone as I wait for the parade of people who will come to remember Janice. Each with their own stories and memories, some more intimate than others. Of how she devilled eggs or wrote on the chalkboard. How she couldn't walk in a straight line if she tried.

I stand frozen, a mannequin in a stockroom, and gaze at my mother's casket. People have arrived and mill around her and somehow she seems increasingly alive. I go to the bathroom, and when I return a group of my mother's friends flock

towards me like I'm a clearance bin. They hug me and squeeze
the tops of my arms. Allison-Jean begins playing the piano
again, and my great-aunt arrives looking like she is from the
old country except for the Sketchers Shape-ups on her feet.
Hair in a bun, green cardigan, round glasses. Within seconds
it is apparent she doesn't know where she is. She walks past
the casket towards the guest book and signs in. A cousin
holds her arm.

"I don't like beef stroganoff," she says. "Do they have anything with chicken?"

By the second visitation I want nothing more to do with
my mother's death.

The next morning is the funeral. We get up early and I make the kids shower. Dan and Allison-Jean will have their kids dressed in formal wear. We strive for shirts that are clean. Glen picks us up and we go to the funeral as a family. The ride to the church is quiet. Wesley finger-draws unknown shapes on the back window and Joan falls asleep, her head tilted a severe ninety degrees.

We file into the front pew. Wes looks around the church.

"Who's that?" He points to an image of Jesus surrounded by sheep on a wall hanging.

"That's Jesus." I whisper.

"Jesus is a *man?*"

Our conversation is cut short by the arrival of the minister. He gives a welcoming address, prays aloud, and invites us to sing an opening hymn. Then he says a few words about my mother's life, her service to the community, her family. He talks about the nature of her death: her proximity to heaven when she passed. How Jesus "had only a short trip to carry her home." I make the mistake of looking at Wes.

"What does that mean?" he asks.

"Grandma died on a plane," I whisper. "So she was already pretty close to heaven."

"And Jesus carried her the rest of the way?"

"Right." I turn my attention back to the altar.

"How?"

"How what?" I whisper.

"How did he carry her? Like in his pocket, or in a back-pack type thing?"

I picture my mother being carried in a giant Baby Bjorn.

"Just in his hands," I tell him. "Now you have to be quiet."

Dan is invited to the altar to deliver the eulogy. He lightens the mood by describing the time my mother chased away an aggressive goose during a family picnic. People enjoy this story.

"So if Grandma had died on a submarine, does that mean she would have been halfway to hell?"

"No, Wes. Shhh . . ." I look at Glen for some assistance, but he is fully engaged in my brother's speech. "Glen," I whisper. But he responds with an outburst of laughter. A joke I have missed.

"Glen!" I say again.

"Can I play on your phone?"

"No, Wes, you cannot play on my phone. We are at Grandma's funeral. Glen!"

He leans in towards me.

"Do something with Wes."

"Come here, bud," he says, pulling him close. "Do you want to play on my phone?"

"I just told him he couldn't play on my phone!"

Joan slithers off the pew. I tell her to get up but she is trying to locate a Smartie that has dropped from her box. Dan looks down from the altar, distracted. We make brief eye contact. His look is one of disappointment. Wes tugs on my arm.

"Give me your phone!"

I shake him off while Glen frantically fumbles for his phone in his pocket, and once located immediately hands it to Wes.

"My mother," Dan begins, "was not an extravagant woman. She took pleasure in the simple things in life: a reliable recipe or the discovery of an interesting shell or a perfectly smooth piece of beach glass. The hundreds of pictures Claudia and I made for her and later those made by her grandchildren." He holds up one of Hannah's horses and presents it slowly from one side of the church to the other. I stare at Hannah's painting. The horse's mane is gnarled and sea-salt-tangled like a runway model's hairdo. The horse is chestnut-coloured. Is this a Sable Island pony? What next Dan? A plane?

Joan retrieves her Smartie and promptly smacks her head on the pew. The loud thud resounds through the church, followed by her high-pitched scream. I scoop her up and press her face into my chest to muffle the noise but it's futile. People look at me sympathetically, except for Dan. I stand to take her out of the church, but Cathy meets me at the end of the pew.

"I'll take her," she says, extending her long arms.

I hand Joan over. She's still crying.

"Can I come too?" Wes asks.

"Go," I reply.

Cathy reaches for Wes's hand. I mouth "thanks" as she ushers my kids down the aisle. Her full-length black skirt swishes behind her.

I hear Wes say, "Yes, I got a new level!" before the door opens and closes.

I slide my sunglasses over my face and cry. Glen offers his hand for comfort. I reach across the space vacated by our kids, and accept it. Dan finishes his eulogy and the minister invites a group of women and a man, who looks like Rex Murphy, to the front of the church. They start singing "Under the Boardwalk." I don't remember this being a part of the service. One of the women is loud and off-key. I look over at my father in the pew across the aisle. The performance causes him to hang his head and cry. He is also loud and competes with the singers. Dan puts an arm around him, gives him a squeeze. His kids sit quietly between him and Allison-Jean like a pair of cardboard cutouts.

I look back up at the group of singers. They sway and the man snaps his fingers. I am irritated that I don't know the significance of the song. After the performance my dad says a few closing words of thanks and the service comes to an end. People begin to file out and "Margo's Cargo" spills into the church from the altar speakers.

Those who share my mother's affinity with Stompin' Tom clap along. Their eyes brighten, their skirts even bounce a little, and they sing. They leave their pews, clad in their brown pantyhose and fall sweaters, and stroll down the aisle. Together they chime in "and Reggie's got the rig!" Margo got the cargo, Reggie the rig, and Janice the coffin. I make sure I don't leave my program behind. Wes, I see, has left a sneaker, jammed in the slot beside the hymnbook. With dirty shoe and program in hand, I'm anxious to escape.

Dan and Dad are already in the aisle. When they pass me, Dan blocks my exit from the pew, pausing to smooth down Dad's lapel. As though he still has an audience. "Go on, now." He says, guiding my father towards the door like he's Rainman.

"I think he knows where the exit is."

"He's exhausted," Dan says.

"Well, we wouldn't even be here if they'd gone to Paris," I say.

Glen and I take the kids trick-or-treating together. It is the first time Joan's really enthusiastic about Halloween and thanks to Allison-Jean's sewing skills, patience, and ability to understand a two-year-old, people get that she is a cat squirrel. House after house she digs around in each shallow aluminum bowl of chocolate bars and fishes out as many as she pleases. The dieters encourage her to take more. They don't want any left behind. They've been snacking all week. Feasting on Kit Kats and Snickers bars during *Coronation Street.* Wesley examines everything that goes into his bag and asks for replacements when he disapproves.

It is under a tree inhabited by a dozen or so plastic ghosts that I realize Glen and I are holding hands. I can feel the scar on his knuckle. Raised and round. A souvenir from a cave tour we took in Bermuda. I don't know how long we've been holding hands or who initiated it and whether I should let go. He doesn't look at me. He keeps his gaze on the house, on our kids begging for chips. I look at him and I don't care that he has back fat or a nose that Joan was unfortunate to inherit. There is something about being held. Even though my hand is the only beneficiary, I feel safe. A chick in an egg. A teapot in bubble wrap.

"I got spicy chips!" Wes calls out to us, jumping down the steps of a house.

"Nice," Glen responds. "Those are my favourite."

Wes drops the Doritos in his pillowcase and cuts across to the next house. "Not on the grass," I yell, waiting for Joan.

A pair of teenagers in *Scream* masks rush past our cat squirrel. Glen moves in and picks her up.

"Grandma," she points to the pair.

"Grandma?" I ask.

"Grandma's a ghost."

"Grandma is not a ghost, Joan."

"Hurry up!" Wes shouts from the end of the next driveway.

The teenagers, who've already been up to the front door and back, pass by us. "Hi, Grandma," Joan says to them.

"No, Joan. Grandma is not a ghost."

"But she in heaven."

"Yes, but she's not there as a serial killer. Frig." I look to Glen for support.

He puts her down at the end of the driveway and straightens her tail. "Grandma's more a spirit. Like a fairy," he explains as an obese Tinkerbell passes by.

"A fairy?" I say, staring at Glen.

"It's better than a ghost," he argues.

"Grandma's a fairy?" Wes asks.

"No!" I interrupt. "She's an angel."

"Is that her over there?" Wes points.

"No. She's not trick-or-treating, okay? She's not here. Grandma's in heaven. Go knock on that door." I point to a house with a trail of pumpkins flanking the front walk.

"Fuck," I say, when they are out of earshot. I root through Joan's bag and jam a mini Oh Henry in my mouth. Glen reaches for my hand. It is more hand pulling than handholding. More "let's go" than "let's be." We follow the kids to the next house. Joan meows, Wes jumps. Still we hold hands until the boys in the *Scream* masks approach and I can't help but think my mother is underneath one. That's when we let go and go back to being two. The boys pass between us, their black cloaks dragging behind them.

Weeks pass.

Dan and I don't talk.

Things with Glen return to the way they were before my mother died: defunct. Our relationship not unlike a human body, a relatively healthy one that climaxed, that created. But inside it always had a flaw you couldn't see but we both knew was there. A heart condition. It slowed us down, tripped us up. When Wes was a baby. When I found out I was pregnant with Joan. We seemed to have it under control; we danced and made things from scratch and for an entire month we had sex and did sixty-nine like we were sixteen. But when Joan began to crawl, so did we, and when she took her first steps, we went into cardiac arrest.

Dad joins a curling club and buys a fancy brush and shoes and tries to set me up with curlers. Some are in their fifties with bodies that look like they've been constructed from Play-Doh. He hangs around the club doing odd jobs other people will have to correct, and he searches for a team in need of a new member. He turns down my Sunday dinner invitations to work charity bonspiels or to watch curling on CBC. Promises of boiled parsnips and mashed turnip don't sway him.

It is not until a Sunday afternoon a week shy of Christmas that he shows up on my doorstep. Wes is playing with a kid down the street when he arrives. They are likely eating snow or playing in the semi-frozen bird bath. Joan is watching a *Little People* DVD we borrowed from Allison-Jean. It features legless clay people with large shoes and chimp-length arms. An Aaron Neville sound-a-like sings the theme song and the characters glide along clay landscapes and help each other.

Dad stands in the entryway holding his curling broom.

"What's for supper?" he asks.

I point to a pineapple on the counter.

"What happened to that turkey dinner you were talking about?"

"That was two weeks ago," I tell him.

He makes a puzzled look as though an acting teacher has instructed him to make a puzzled look. "Really?"

"Really."

He shrugs and hangs his coat in the closet and says, "Where's my Joanie?" in a bear-like voice. She giggles and Aaron Neville introduces the next character in need of encouragement and I wonder if the show's writers ever wish they had more creative freedom. That they could substitute themes of friendship and self-esteem with secret clay people fight clubs and playground poker.

I rummage through the cupboards and find a taco kit. It will have to work. I can hear my cellphone ringing in the bedroom but I ignore it and put a package of ground beef in the microwave to defrost. Wes comes through the door breathing heavily and yells, "Grandpa!"

"Take your boots off first," I say, as Wes tramps down the hall towards the living room. Each boot comes off with a thump before he leaps onto the couch. Dad groans under his weight and Joan proceeds to kick.

"Joan, stop kicking," I yell, as I cut an inch of mould off

the cheese and hide it under a layer of onion skin in the garbage. I will grate the cheese into a bowl and serve it to my family, though I myself will not be putting cheese on my taco.

Wesley takes a second to watch *Little People,* then he announces that the show sucks, turns off the DVD player, and changes the channel, so Joan pulls the remote from him and hits him with it. He cries and she starts to cry and Dad quickly gets up from the couch to observe and I realize that the writers of the *Little People* are probably parents and that they write about harmonious idyllic things because in reality fight clubs exist in their living rooms too.

"Timeout! Both of you."

Joan seems okay with this and sits on the rubber mat. Wesley is less receptive and spends several seconds howling into a pillow. I grab his arm, which is skinny and cool from the outdoors, and pull him up from the couch. He refuses to place his feet on the ground and I nearly drop him. A piece of shredded cheese falls from my shirt onto his forehead, which he accuses me of throwing at him. I glance at Joan who is bent over, biting her big toenail.

"Stop that! That's disgusting."

Wesley breaks free and jumps onto the couch.

I hear the front door open, and go to check who else has arrived. Like Thing 1 and Thing 2, Dan's kids are at the door standing at attention beside their ride-on Trunki suitcases.

"Hi," I greet them. Dan is behind them on the step.

"Hi Auntie Claudia," Hannah says.

"Allison's in labour," Dan says, out of breath. "Contractions are really close. I tried to call." It is the first time I have seen him since the funeral. He looks fatter. We avoid eye contact.

"Good luck," I say.

He nods and gives quick hugs to his kids before rushing

back to the car where Allison-Jean is shifting up and down in her seat like a kettlebell is about to swing out of her crotch.

Dad rushes up behind me. "Good luck, Danny! Hurry hard!"

We both wave, and I return to the kitchen.

"Would anyone like a drink?" I ask, trying to remember the feeling when the kettlebell finally comes out and you see it for the first time. Wes asks for pop, Joan picks her nose and eats it.

"I will have a glass of milk," Hannah says politely.

"Me too," Liam says, raising his hand.

"Looks like you've got your hands full," Dad chuckles, filling a glass with tap water.

I flash him a dirty look, remove the now partially cooked ground beef from the microwave, drop it into a pan, and start frying it.

"We don't have any pop, Wesley."

"Then give me orange juice."

"Is that how you ask?"

He says, "Please," while making a ridiculous face that doesn't amuse me.

"Do you mind getting them drinks?" I ask my father.

He says, "Of course not."

A minute later Wesley says, "This is yucky," and spits his juice on the coffee table.

His cousins enjoy this type of behaviour because it is foreign to them. Particularly Hannah who is six going on twelve.

I tell him to clean it up. Argue that there is nothing wrong with the juice, though upon closer observation notice it's cloudy. I take it to the kitchen.

"Did you notice anything funny about the juice?" I say to my father, holding the cup up to the light.

"I just mixed in a little apple juice," he explains, putting a handful of cheese in his mouth. "There was only a bit left."

"But we don't mix juice."

"I just didn't want to see it go to waste."

I say nothing but try to determine why he assumed the apple juice would go to waste. Does he mix the juice at Dan's house? Is their juice also at risk of going to waste? Are all juices at risk of going to waste? I chop a tomato, count to ten the way my mother would, and stir the meat.

"We don't mix juice," I say again.

"Don't worry about it," he says. "You don't have to apologize."

I count to ten, in Mandarin this time, and I think of Alphonse Jr. and how peaceful he looked dead.

"Say, what did you do with the roosters?" he asks, pointing at the border. "Your mother loved those darn things. Especially those ones." He gestures to one of the remaining mug shot roosters. "Did you know that's the reason she put the border up in the living room?"

"No, Dad. I did not know that." I set the table, and then I slip out the back door for fresh air.

Later that night, Allison-Jean pushes out a girl in sixteen minutes.

I take the next day off work. Dad comes back to babysit all the kids when I go to the hospital. After arriving and realizing I'm empty-handed, I duck into the gift shop. The selection is limited to overpriced stuffed animals, Willow Tree statues, and Glosette raisins.

The man behind the cash says, "Can I help you?" He wears a name tag and a blue pin with volunteer typed in bold letters.

"Just looking for a gift," I reply, stopping at a rack of bibs that say Spit Happens.

"Boy or a girl?"

"Girl."

The bibs don't amuse me. They amuse middle-aged women with tight perms and turtlenecks.

"How about music?"

He points to a collection of CDs by a Pepsi machine.

I glance over the display and pick one featuring Celtic lullabies, then go back and choose a Spit Happens bib because it will likely also appeal to piano teachers like Allison-Jean.

"Will that be everything?" the volunteer asks.

"That's it."

He rings the stuff in and jams the items into a tiny bag. I stop and pick up a coffee at a Tim Horton's kiosk before heading up to the fifth floor. The elevator is crowded and smells like fish. People around me sniff. Then the elevator dings and opens a few feet below the fifth floor.

"Well that doesn't happen every day!" says a man wearing a Proud Grandpa T-shirt.

A doctor opens the compartment containing the emergency phone and everyone glances in, expecting to see an octopus or something, but there is nothing in there, except the phone, which is covered in tape and not working. He sighs and presses the emergency button eleven times. I know it's eleven because I count and it makes me wonder if he has inside information that indicates the button has to be pressed specifically eleven times so that we all warp to level six and start clubbing turtles.

The elevator shakes a bit and seems to lose power.

"We're going to have to climb out," a nurse says. She finishes eating a tea biscuit then moves to the front of the pack.

"Some help?" she requests.

The proud grandpa hikes up his pants and goes down on one knee. The nurse promptly steps on it and hoists herself up. Then she says, "Next," and a woman takes off her drippy snow boots and, also with the help of the grandpa's knee, and the nurse's extended hand, frees herself up to the fifth floor. The doctor politely declines the grandpa's knee or anyone's help, and he awkwardly clambers up and out on his own. One by one the elevator empties of its passengers. The grandpa grunts under the weight of a hefty woman in a lab coat. She looks embarrassed as she rolls onto the fifth floor.

It's my turn at last, and just in time because it feels like the area is getting smaller and I might do something rash to distract myself like nibble the carpet or hang upside down from the safety bars lining the elevator's perimeter. The grandpa tells me to "hop on."

When I hurl myself onto the fifth floor, I land at my brother's feet. He looks down at me and the puddle of drool that shot out of my mouth on impact, pauses as though thinking of something to say, then turns and goes down the hall.

"Spit happens," I holler after him as I pull myself to my feet. He shakes his head and rounds the corner.

The grandpa calls up from the elevator shaft, a little exasperated, "A little help down here?" and an orderly comes to his rescue.

I walk down the hall, where women with gnarly robes and engorged breasts roam around looking for ice chips and free muffins, and arrive at Allison-Jean's room. The baby is ten pounds. They've named her Emma. She is bald and wears a frilly dress and matching socks.

"Why don't you put her in a sleeper?" I suggest to Dan. "Don't you think she'd be more comfortable?"

"She's having her picture taken," he says irritably. He, understandably, looks tired.

"Your breath stinks," I tell him.

He looks at me but says nothing as Allison-Jean emerges from the bathroom. I tell her congratulations. She looks like a drug addict. Her face is covered in broken blood vessels. She picks up a stack of papers and begins filling them out with a pen when a nurse comes in the room with painkillers. I wish it were like communion and we could all take part. Dan hands her water and she swallows the contents of the cup loudly.

"How's your pain?" the nurse asks.

"About a five," Allison-Jean responds.

They continue to converse and the nurse nods and records things on a chart and I spy through the curtain at the patient next door. Her face is puffy and pale and she has broken blood vessels along her jaw line like Allison-Jean. Her baby sits next to her in a plastic bin. I wonder if she is alone.

"Did you hear what I said?" Dan asks.

The girl's arm is long and stick-like. It appears she is reaching for her glasses.

"What?"

"I said her middle name is JANICE."

"Right." *Oh Danny, you shouldn't have.*

Dan shakes his head and Emma begins to whimper and I can only assume it's because just hours ago she had to travel out of Allison-Jean's vagina, and now she's been forced to wear a small headband that looks like a garter.

"Don't you want to hold her?"

Allison-Jean appears to have fallen asleep in six seconds. Her mouth is open.

"Do I want to?" I reply, stunned. "Yes, of course I want to hold her."

Emma is all face. Her cheeks spill out over her eyes and chin. There is a lot of her.

"She's adorable," I say, gently unwrapping the receiving blanket to examine the rest of her features. Her shoulders are furry. Dan scooches in beside me on the heater I'm using as a seat.

"Allison-Jean disagrees, but I think she looks like Liam," he says.

My brother and I stare at his offspring. The only one who will never know her grandma. It makes me sad. Soon enough, Joan probably won't remember her. I am thinking about this, attempting to re-swaddle Emma, when her lips curl into the shape of a smile. It only lasts for a second, but my brother and I both see it. We look at each other.

"Mom," we say, together.

When I arrive home from the hospital the house is a mess. Dad is watching curling highlights on TSN and criticizing Kevin Martin.

"Where are the kids?"

Dad points ambiguously.

"Where?"

"They're having a bath."

"All of them?"

"They wanted to."

"Dad, Joan can't take a bath unsupervised!"

I charge down the hall to the bathroom. All four kids are jammed in the tub. Bottles of shampoo and conditioner float between them. Their labels have been picked off. The water is cool. Liam is blue.

"Did Grandpa wash your hair?" I ask, fingering through Joan's dreadlocks.

"Look at this, Mommy," Wes says, holding up a wrestler. "I pulled his head off."

"Why would you do that?" I ask, irritated.

I can hear Dad cheering from the hall. He says, "Come look at this replay!"

"I'm trying to get the kids out of the tub."

"You're going to miss it!"

"That's okay," I assure him.

I hear him clapping as I lift the kids out one at a time and towel them off. I brush my kids' teeth and give Dan's kids dental floss. After I dress Wes and Joan in their pajamas, I tell them to go pick out a book. Hannah and Liam dress themselves. I give them my bed.

"Check it out," my father says, pointing to the TV. "Watch this shot."

"Emma has Mom's mouth."

Dad looks away from the screen. His posture falls apart.

"Sorry," I say. "But you have to see her."

He covers his face in a childlike way. But I don't have time for another child.

"Did you feed them?" I glance at the clock in the kitchen, it's 7:30.

"We had microwaved English muffins, cheese slices and some of that left-over chicken."

Who microwaves English muffins? I look at Wes, sitting at Dad's feet with a Hot Wheels. I go into my bathroom to restock the toilet paper and feel exhausted. Other people's grief. The new baby. I won't have another baby. I begin digging through my drawers behind vials of separated foundation and purse tampons for my stash of cigarettes — the menthols I occasionally smoke on weekends when the kids are with Glen. There are two left in the pack. I remove one and conceal it in my hand.

When I return to the living room, Dad is explaining curling to Wes, who grinds his teeth between saying, intermittently, "Peep!"

"Are you peeping?" I ask him, to which my eldest responds, "Peep."

"Do you have a piece of paper?" Dad asks.

"On the second shelf," I reply, nodding in its direction.

He gets the paper and begins drawing a sheet of ice. "This is the hog line," he points.

"Peep!"

"Stop peeping!" I yell. "I have to run out and get some milk. Do you mind watching the kids for a bit longer?"

Of course Dad does not mind because I get TSN and he has basic cable.

"Go ahead."

"Thanks." I put my boots on and pick my coat up off the floor.

Wes walks by the entryway and says, "Peep."

"STOP peeping. Did anyone see my keys?"

"Me come!" Joan says.

"Mommy will only be gone for a minute."

"Peep."

"Wes! Dad — have you seen my keys?"

"Sorry honey, I haven't." He moves to the edge of the couch, drawn to the TV. "Yes!" he raises his arms in victory.

"Peep."

"Where the hell are my keys?"

Wes points to his room. I remove my boots and my left sock gets stuck so I throw the left boot angrily into the hall closet and call it a bitch.

I find my keys on Wes's bed. I sit down momentarily to count to ten and there to my left on his bedside table are Wes's wrestling figurines, each with a cigarette taped to his plastic lips. Eight wrestlers smoking. Wes stands in the doorway. He yells, "Peep!" and runs into the kitchen. I sit down on the bed. Joan runs in and yells, "Peep!"

In the living room a commercial break comes on playing "The Twelve Days of Christmas."

I sing in my head, *Two peeping children, and a mo-ther-er in a pear —*

Fuck. I still haven't put up a tree.

Our artificial tree leans to the left. Despite hours of searching, I can't find the box of Christmas decorations. So we improvise, hanging popcorn strings and household items: a stainless steel strainer, salad tongs, and a whisk. It looks like a dollar store. I take a corkscrew off the tree and open a bottle of wine to celebrate the beginning of Christmas vacation. Wes takes a small sip.

"Tastes like dog poop."

"Have you tasted dog poop?" I ask him.

"No!" he says, amused.

"Well then how do you know it tastes like dog poop?"

"Because it is dog poop."

"Right, that makes a lot of sense."

"Sometimes dogs eat their poop," Wes continues.

"Yes, that is sometimes the case."

"George eats his poop."

"Who's George?" I ask.

"Daddy's new dog."

"Your dad doesn't have a dog."

Joan pipes in and says, "Yes he does."

"Since when?"

Wes shrugs and Joan says since "last year," which in her brain could mean ten seconds or a month. She then corrects herself, holds up six fingers, and says, "Thirty pounds."

"He got it when Grandma got killed."

"Grandma didn't *get killed,* Wes. She *passed away.*"

"What does that mean?"

"It means she died."

"That's what I said. She got killed."

I re-clip Joan's hair and ask her what George looks like.

"He brown."

"He's brown?"

"And he nice."

"Well that's good to know." I kiss her head before she joins her brother on the couch. I top off my wine and phone Glen. Outside it starts to snow.

"Hey."

"Hey." He pauses. "What's up?"

"Nothing. We just finished decorating the tree and the kids mentioned you got a dog."

"Yeah. George."

"Oh."

"I thought I told you that months ago."

"No."

"Oh . . . is that it?"

"I was also wondering what you got the kids for Christmas." I'm hoping he didn't go overboard this year. I unwrap a cranberry brie from the freezer and turn on the oven. Joan and Wes begin assembling a fort out of couch cushions and blankets.

Glen says, "I was thinking of getting them ski lessons."

"Ski lessons? Joan's not even three."

"It's never too early."

"You don't even ski."

"Yes, I do."

"Since when?"

"I've skied for years."

"Well, I think that's weird."

I hang up and get drunk in the fort so I don't have to think about Glen. Ski Glen. Latte Glen. Dog Glen. I want the original Glen. The familiar one that likes Canadian Tire flyers and chocolate milk. The one with parenting suggestions I can dismiss or plans I can kibosh. The one I can control. New, separated Glen has hobbies and opinions like new Barbie. Pet Vet Barbie. Pancake Chef Barbie. I down the rest of my wine and lie like a starfish on the living room floor. The kids fall asleep on either side of me. Whatever happened to just plain old slutty Barbie?

It's Christmas Eve, but it seems more like a terrorist attack is pending. Crowds gather at Walcrotch to buy one of everything. I join the masses and search for a turkey. Allison-Jean comes without the baby. We meet near the optometrist's cubby hole and divide the Christmas grocery list in half. Wes asks if he can have glasses.

Then Dad calls and insists on meeting me there. He has not done any Christmas shopping. I'm frustrated. This is going to hold me up. I tell him to find me in the toy department. When he does, he looks frazzled. There are water droplets on his glasses and he's wearing one of my mother's toques.

"Sorry," he says. "I couldn't find a parking spot."

"Or a hat," I say.

He pulls off the angora toque and stuffs it in his pocket. The bottom third of his pants are wet. He notices me staring at them.

"I couldn't find my boots either. Where are my grand-kids?" he asks.

"They're looking at Christmas decorations with Allison-Jean. She's helping me get stuff for dinner. Who do you have left to buy for?" I ask.

"Just the kids."

Overflowing carts manoeuvre noisily around us. A pair of legwarmers gets stuck on the wheel of my cart and I push them around.

"That's not bad," I say. "I thought you said you hadn't done any shopping. Any ideas of what you'd like to get them?"

"Not a clue. Your mother would always pick out stuff for the kids."

"Okay," I say. "Let's start with the baby."

We cruise to the baby aisle and he picks out some pastel coloured blocks for Emma and a singing bear. He is proud.

"Should I get her something else . . . I mean, is this enough?"

"I think what you have is fine."

We amble up and down the toy aisles. My father loads up the cart with plastic things as Salvation Army bells jingle in the distance. When he's finished I lead him back to the grocery section. I see Allison-Jean near the bananas. Joan is in the cart. Wesley stands close to her side and stares at an obese person driving a scooter.

"Why don't you go pay for this stuff so the kids don't see?"

He agrees and takes possession of the cart.

"Other way," I call after him.

The produce department is busy. Middle-aged people guide their elderly parents around and ask them loud questions about root vegetables and if the parents don't respond quickly enough their middle-aged children make executive decisions — yes to the turnip, no to the parsnip.

Wesley is still staring at the man driving through the bakery on a scooter.

"Is that the guy from *Wall-E?*"

"No, Wes."

Joan points to a bin of chocolate in the bulk section. "Can me have some of dis?"

I say, "No," and she starts whining.

"Why?"

"Because there are bugs in there."

She stares at me suspiciously. "What kind of bugs?"

"Ones with wings and yellow eyes."

"Can me see those bugs?"

"No," I reason, "they are too small."

They are too small the way the bugs on all of the Dora the Explorer toys are too aggressive, too fast on the Timbits, too poisonous on the coin-operated bus in the mall food court. She stops whining and stares at the chocolate. I add a giant bag of potatoes to the cart, aware I should stop using the bug excuse.

Can I go to Grandpa's?

No.

Why? Because he has bugs?

We finish the rest of the groceries and join a line three carts deep. Dad has finished paying and waves at us. He is in the way of people trying to get to the McDonald's. I offer to give Allison-Jean money since I am supposed to be hosting dinner, but she refuses. She pulls into the checkout beside me. Her post-partum cart is not orderly and she loads things onto the belt with a certain recklessness. Tins of cranberry sauce, loaves of white bread for stuffing. Her short hair stands straight up. It occurs to me that I don't really know her that well. I know her as someone who can sew, take family photos, and play piano, when we need her to. But in this moment of can tossing, not surrounded by her three kids and Dan, I sort of want to know more.

The man in front of me watches the conveyor belt intently and when vacant space appears he taps the person in front of him and points. The lady shrugs off his tapping and hoists her ham up onto the belt. It rocks back and forth and leaks. He takes a step forward and prepares to unload his basket the second space becomes available so that he may immediately line up his endives. There's a pleased shriek to my right, which shifts my attention to Joan who has ripped the covers off four different magazines. I pretend she hasn't and hide them in a discarded shopping basket.

It is snowing by the time we reach the parking lot. The flakes are large and all three of us instinctively stick out our tongues. My mother loved this type of snow. Quiet snow, she would call it. Heavy and silent. I load the kids and the groceries into the car. The nearest cart corral is full. As I look for a place to ditch the cart, someone interrupts my search and asks if he could use it.

"Sure," I say, turning around. I hand the cart off to someone I briefly dated in university. We share an awkward look. Uncomfortable familiarity. He reaches for the cart, nods his thanks, and he and a woman in a brown coat make their way towards the store. I feel nothing but the damp cuffs of my Joe Fresh pants and a sudden pang of loneliness. My mother isn't coming for Christmas dinner and neither is Glen.

I start the car, reverse into the fray of shoppers, and begin the slow exit from the parking lot. My dad cuts in line in front of me, with a little wave. He's wearing my mother's purple angora hat again, and attempts to make a left-hand turn from the right lane. Honking ensues.

The kids ask to play outside when we get home. I exchange wet mittens for dry ones and send them into the backyard. As I'm putting the groceries away, even though it's 11:00 a.m., I open a Corona. It doesn't seem quite right with the snow, or the hour. But it's completely refreshing. Cathy calls and asks to come over. I welcome the company. She will see the afternoon as a project.

Now that I have *real* ornaments I'm able to swap them on the tree for a combination lock and a set of wooden spoons. The top of the tree remains vacant. This will need to be remedied.

I settle into the couch with my beer, telling myself I can take a break until Cathy arrives. *The First 48* is on TV. Someone finds a body hog-tied in an alleyway. A man in his fifties with pink feet. There's an old mattress nearby with gold thread that catches the sunlight. It's in Miami. The investigators arrive on the scene and notice bugs on the mattress. I shiver and glance out the sliding door at the backyard. The kids are building a snowman.

"Hello?" Cathy sings from the front door.

"Come in," I call.

She hangs her coat in the closet and removes her boots.

"Grab a beer, there's lime on the counter."

She swings open the fridge and takes one.

"Where are the kids?"

"In the backyard."

She pokes her lime wedge into her bottle and licks her fingers.

"I brought presents," she says, cheerily.

"I told you not to get anything."

"Yeah, I know, but I had to."

She joins me in the living room, stands at the sliding door. "Do you know Wes is using your barbecue brush as a shovel?"

"Yes."

I get up from the couch and join her, watching the kids. Joan waves and eats snow off her mitten. Highway traffic can be heard in the distance: acceleration, and uprooted slush smacking the pavement. The air is moist and dense. Perfect for colouring cheeks and carrying reindeer.

I slide the door open a crack and call, "Come inside! Cathy has presents for you."

There is a foot race to the door. Joan pulls off Wes's boot.

"Get your boot."

Wes reluctantly goes back for his boot and both clamber in the house, dumping their boots beside the mat. Cathy helps them remove layers of wet clothing. I make hot chocolate. On the TV the hog-tied body resembles the turkey I just bought for Christmas dinner. It is moved to the morgue where it will spend Christmas alone. I shut off the TV as Cathy kneels on the floor and hands Wes and Joan each a present. Both are covered in bows. They each open a pair of Zhu Zhu pets. Wes jumps up and down.

"Can we open them now?" he asks. Joan has already started biting the cardboard.

"Sure," I say.

Cathy frees both sets of mechanical hamsters and puts them on the floor. They chirp and spin in circles, moving left and right until they hit a wall and start spinning again. The kids laugh incessantly while I dodge the hamsters. Cathy collects the packaging and hands it to me. I toss it in the recycling bin under the sink.

"Can you figure out a way to hang these?" I ask, passing her a limp stack of stockings. "I can't find the things that go on the mantle."

"Sure," she replies, getting up off the floor. She rifles through my junk drawer, while I haul out ingredients for cookies. "I'm seeing a naturopath next week."

"Are your allergies acting up again?"

"No, I'm having a cleanse. I read this article on Yahoo that said our colons are the most toxic parts of our body."

"So what, do you have to take a bunch of pills?"

"No, the pills don't work. Using a pill would be like flushing your engine with hand soap. It's called colon hydrotherapy."

I don't know what colon hydrotherapy entails, but I picture a bum running through a sprinkler.

"They basically run water through your colon to clean it out."

"Can't you just sit on a hose?" I ask.

Cathy tips her head back and finishes her beer. I take her empty. "There's more to it than that. There are special breathing techniques you have to follow. And massage. It's going to take at least five sessions, if not more."

"A fire hose then. Sit on a fire hose and breath heavy."

"Claudia," Cathy sighs. "It's all about function. Making sure all the parts work."

"Cathy, I'm lucky if I remember to brush my teeth in the morning."

"Can we have more marshmallows?" Wes asks, stirring his hot chocolate with his hand.

I grab the bag from the cupboard and dump marshmallows

in the kids' mugs. The Zhu Zhu pets have stopped. Cathy collects the four of them and places them in a line. Depresses their backs to set them into motion. They split; all go in different directions and find open space, except for a spotted one. It repeatedly smacks into the dishwasher and goes in circles. Maybe it needs its colon cleansed.

Mid-afternoon, Cathy leaves and Glen picks up the kids. He's giving me a couple of hours of peace before dinner at his place. Chinese food, because it's what we used to have on Christmas Eve. I tell him I'll be there at six.

When his car is out of sight, I haul the kids' presents from the closet and spread them out over the living room floor. I can't find the Scotch tape I bought specifically for wrapping presents, but I find a roll of medical tape and two rolls of masking tape in the junk drawer. I wrap until my neck is sore and I realize I've overspent again. On LEGO, big-eyed stuffies, and a fifty-dollar parchment-paper Rapunzel dress. New carpet will have to wait.

I make coffee with eggnog, take it to the living room, then I decide to take it right out to the back deck, where I stand in the snow in my slippers. I shield my eyes from the sun. Suddenly, a pair of deer emerges from the woods at the edge of our yard. They are not strangers. They are camels, according to Joan, and both girls.

I watch them get closer and agree they look feminine. Acutely alert and maternal with dainty ears and breath, I imagine, that is warm and slightly sweet, like a pancake. I am reminded of the time Glen went hunting and lied about it. The Lady's Slipper he brought back and stuck in a mason jar. I called him an asshole while Wes stood in his crib biting the rails, and Glen told me to fuck off and tipped over a lamp. It was nothing like the early years when we had sex in the shower, and afterwards made couscous.

The doorbell rings and one of the deer lifts her head as though she heard it too. I go to the front door where my father stumbles in and lands on his knees in the entryway. I check my watch. It is just 5:00 p.m.

"What are you doing here?" I ask, alarmed.

He hoists one leg up and grabs the doorknob for assistance.

"Sorry," he replies, pulling himself up in a roundabout way.

"What's going on?" I ask again. "Did you drive here?"

I step around him to see if his car is in the driveway, but there's a cab. The driver is outside, leaning against his car. He waves at me.

"What?"

"Ten dollars!"

I get my purse and find the Scotch tape jammed into the side pocket. I run out, pay the driver in change, and he hands me a large bag of wrapped gifts my father left in the back seat. When I come back inside, my father is stretched out on the couch with his pants undone.

"What's wrong with you?"

He says, "Rum," and closes his eyes.

"Rum?"

Then the phone rings and it's Dan, asking if I've seen him.

"Yes," I reply, "he dropped by earlier with some presents."

"Do you know where he is now?"

"No," I lie. "Why?"

My dad rights himself on the couch.

"Because he was supposed to be here for four."

"What time is it now?" I fake surprise at the hour. "He's probably lost track of time without Mom."

Dan hesitates, then he asks, "You're not alone, are you? For dinner?"

"No, Dan. I'm having dinner with Glen and the kids."

"Okay," he replies.

There is a period of silence I use to examine the calluses on my feet.

"Merry Christmas, Dan."

I hang up and find my dad washing his face in the bathroom.

"You were supposed to be at Dan's an hour ago."

"What?" he asks, wringing out the washcloth.

"You should be at Dan's! He just called looking for you."

I feel like I'm having a conversation with Wesley.

"But I thought . . ." He stops and scrunches his forehead and I can see that he is trying to organize his thoughts as though they are little primary-coloured blocks.

"Oh geez, can you pass me my shoes, honey?"

"Where are you going?"

"I was supposed to be at Dan's at four."

"Yes, but you can't go to Dan's smelling like that. He would freak out."

He looks at me blankly. Like someone knocked over the blocks. I go to the linen closet and pull out an extra toothbrush with a rubber Spiderman clinging to the handle.

"Use this."

He obliges and returns to the bathroom. Thinking for a moment, I go into the kitchen and pour the rest of the coffee from the pot into a thermos and hand it to him.

"For the road."

"But I just brushed my teeth."

"Let's *go*."

I motion for the door. Dad rummages through the bag of presents, takes ours out, and ties off the bag. "These ones are for Dan."

I carry the presents to the tree. Most are wrapped in the green cellophane my mother used to wrap her Christmas cakes in. The sticky labels are the ones for jam, with berries in the corners. At least he made the effort; he used Scotch tape. My gift, I note, is in a tissue-less bag covered with Easter eggs.

By the time we get to my brother's, Dad's drunk the coffee, and seems to have sobered up. Or, at least, appears to be sober. I stop to let him off a few doors down, but I can see Allison-Jean standing in the window. She is partially obscured by oversized snowflake cutouts that hang in their window. Dad says thanks and goes to open the car door.

"Don't forget the presents," I remind him.

"Oh yes," he says, and I hand him the bag of gifts, which he obediently carries carefully, one hand on the bottom.

"I'll see you tomorrow."

He nods and I drive away feeling pathetic and proud, like the parent, not the child, the mother, not the daughter.

There's no sense going home before Glen's, but if I drive there directly from dropping Dad off I'll be there early. And we agreed on six, so he could have time with the kids by himself. So I drive to a house in the west end that boasts a thousand or so Christmas lights to see if it's worth the trip. If so, I will take the kids on the way home from dinner.

The weather is mild and lots of people are out walking. No one is carolling.

I can't get close to the house because there are cars lining both sides of the road, so I park a few streets away and walk over. A fervent couple show off the display to their single over-dressed toddler, who is too young and could care less about the blinking Santa. He would rather eat rocks or suck on his foot. His parents won't get this until he's three and they see he's capable of getting it. Which makes me think: Wes will get it. Will Joan? I'll wait until next year when they both get it.

I return to my car and smell weed in the vicinity. It takes me back to my university days. When you could still smoke in the bars. Before there were iPhone apps that could check your pulse. Before people had heard about BPA or worried about swine flu. Before I wore clothes I bought in a grocery store. A pair of young men smoke openly across the street. They see me staring and the shorter of the two holds up the joint. I cross towards them. The joint is small, the paper wrinkled, the amount left almost negligible. I receive it carefully, pinch the end and inhale. It tastes as I remember. Vaguely organic, yet off. Brown sugar on the burner. I turn my back to a passing SUV and take a second haul. The smoke, trapped in my closed mouth, encircles my tongue slowly and seductively. I hand the joint back, pull a piece of wool off my lip, and go back to my car already stoned. One of the men yells, "Ciao." They carry on as though I'd never been there.

I feel everything and nothing. Nauseous and light. Like I could dance on pointe shoes or drive a tractor. Pass out or climb a tree.

I arrive at Glen's a shade past six and work hard on smiling just the right amount.

"Hi," he says, opening the door.

"Hi," I reply, passing him my coat. I notice my face in the front hall mirror and realize I got the smile wrong. I resemble the woman who had plastic surgery to look like a cat. Glen wears grey wool pants and an argyle sweater. He looks exceptional.

"You okay?"

"Yes," I assure him. "Just in the spirit."

"The *Christmas* spirit?" he asks closely.

I ignore him.

"Mommy!" Wes yells. He charges over nearly knocking me to the ground. "Come see what I got!"

"I let them each open a present," Glen says. "I'll send the rest with you."

"Stop staring at me," I say, and turn my attention to Wes, who produces a tank-type thing with monster-truck wheels and a strobe light.

"What the hell kind of light is that?"

He makes shooting noises and spit flies from his mouth. Joan sits in the corner brushing the periwinkle-blue hair of a new My Little Pony. Every once in a while she smacks it hard with the brush. I watch her play fixedly and find myself clapping when she hits it.

"Why are you clapping?" Glen asks, confused.

He sets the table. I kneel on the floor and sit on my hands.

"Come show me your piny," I say to Joan.

She stares at me.

"What?"

Wes's monster truck passes between us.

"I want to see your piny."

My family stare down at me from varying heights and make me feel dizzy.

"What?" I repeat.

"I think we should eat," Glen says. "Maybe you can see the piny after dinner."

He tells the kids to wash their hands and goes out back. His steps are extra heavy. Like he's trying to tenderize the floor. I pick myself up off the ground and take a seat at the table. Glen returns a minute later with a dog. It comes straight to the table and jams his head into my lap.

"This must be George," I say, though I want to call it Jombi.

"It is." Glen slaps his thigh. "Come here, George." The dog saunters over, nails clicking on the hardwood floor. "Who's a good boy?" Glen scratches George affectionately behind the ears and praises him. I watch longingly. *I'm a good boy!*

We eat dinner in the dining room, which I observe has been redone. The walls are deep brown with a metallic sheen, I wager expensive paint. There are large pieces of abstract artwork hanging on the walls. Joan picks peas from her fried rice.

"Don't put them in the butter dish," Glen sighs.

I begin to feel less stoned. A sudden change in altitude. An

airplane making its final descent. I remove a wonton from a
paper bag and balance it on the edge of my plate. Glen slides
me a glass of water. The wine, which had been previously set
to the right of my place setting, has been relocated, full, to the
kitchen counter. I pretend not to notice. Wes dips his fingers
in the plum sauce.

"What's with the art?" I ask Glen, pointing to his paintings with my fork.

"This series of mine is called *In Contempt.*"

"You did these?"

He nods.

I am unable to process the name and what it might mean
in relation to the images because I am hung up on the fact that
he now paints "series" and that his "series" have names and
there are so many lines. Hundreds of thousands of lines. As
though all of the world's subway maps have been transferred
on top of each other.

"What do you think?"

"I like them," I say, desiring a nap. I swallow a chicken ball
whole. It passes painfully down my esophagus like a glacier
over a rock, slow and immense. I hold my neck.

"Are you okay?" Glen partially stands, alarmed.

"Yes," I squeak out. "It just went down the wrong way."

Joan excuses herself from the table. I wipe tears from my
eyes and reach for my water.

"So you really like them?"

I am no longer high. The plane has landed, finished its taxi,
and I am stuck in the back row waiting to de-plane, wishing
I hadn't taken the flight in the first place.

"Yes. Though I think the middle one may be a tad too
busy."

"Really?" He ponders this for a bit. "Even despite the title?"

I don't know what he means by this. I can only think of contempt in the context of someone being in contempt of court.

"Yes. Even despite the title." I want George to put his head on my lap again. I want him to make me feel better. And I still want to call him Jombi. I also have a compelling urge to suck my thumb. I don't ever want to smoke weed again.

"That one was going to be your Christmas present," Glen says, disappointed.

I smile. "I still like it," I say, taking the last egg roll. "How did you learn to paint like that?"

"I took a class."

"Can I be finished?" Wesley asks.

Glen tells him to eat two more pieces of broccoli. Wes obliges then excuses himself. Joan emerges from beneath the table and follows her brother. The TV comes on in the next room.

"Are you drunk?" Glen asks.

"No," I say defensively. "I'm just tired."

"It's Christmas Eve," he argues.

"I'm NOT drunk!"

"Well you're acting like it." He brushes rice from the table into his hand and dumps it into the paper bag.

"I was stoned."

"Oh, that's nice," he says sarcastically.

"What are you implying, Glen?"

"I'm *implying* nothing. I'm stating it's inappropriate that you'd show up here all fucked up."

"You were drunk when I delivered Joan."

"That was different."

"Stop fighting!" Wes calls from the other room.

"We're not fighting!" I attempt to assure him. "How was that different?"

"I came from a golf tournament."

"Yes, and you knew there was a good chance I was in labour that morning."

"You didn't call me until you were six centimetres."

"Four."

I get up from the table and grab the bottle of wine from the kitchen counter. Glen does not follow. I hear him blow out the candles and stack plates. I don't even want the wine. I stand with my back to the fridge and try not to cry. Wes pads softly into the kitchen.

"*The Polar Express* is coming on next!" he says.

"That's good," I say. "Go quick before you miss it."

He runs back to the TV room. I put the wine down and start searching through the cupboards for tea. Glen asks what I'm looking for and points to a drawer when I tell him. Then he joins the kids.

"Daddy look! It's coming on."

I sit hunched over my mug feeling diminished and small. George still hasn't come to make me feel better. I see him down the hall eating a pig's ear. I hate Glen, but I look up and there he is, standing in the kitchen's entrance with his hands in his pockets.

"Sorry," he mutters. "I never really considered how hard this must be."

"I want my mom."

"I know you do."

His phone buzzes from his pocket.

"Go ahead," I say.

He disappears down the hall. I hear his bedroom door close. Tea sloshes from my mug as I carry it to the living room and park myself in front of the *Polar Express* between Wes and Joan. Tom Hanks is everywhere. If his fucking volleyball shows up, I'm leaving.

Christmas morning goes off without a hitch. We sleep in until eight then open our stockings, which are made of red felt and have our names along the cuffs in glitter glue. The "G" has been removed from Glen's and is used for Optimus Prime, who gets a box of Tic Tacs and Transformer Band-Aids. Mine contains a juice box straw and a pair of earrings Wes has taken from my bedroom. I make a big deal about the earrings then move on to the presents under the tree.

We are not methodical. Paper is ripped and bags dumped out. Clothes are tossed like they were received in error. My children look like meth addicts in search of a hit. Wes gets a paper cut and the medical tape I used to wrap their presents comes in handy.

"Who's this one for?" Wes asks, holding up a present.

"That's for me," I say, reading the label, "from Grandpa."

Wes returns to the tree and I open my present.

"What is it?" Wes asks, picking his nose.

I flip over the box. "It's a Perfect Meatloaf Pan."

"What's a meatloaf pan?"

"A pan that makes meatloaf."

"Why?"

I have no explanation for him. Not for the pan or for the reason it was given to me.

"What do you guys want for breakfast?"

They agree on scrambled eggs. I serve them with ketchup

and sliced oranges and pour myself a second cup of coffee. I
catch Wes trying to open a packaged Star Wars figurine with
a steak knife.

"Put that back!" I yell. "I'll open it in a minute. Frig."

I take a scoop of birdseed and a handful of peanuts out
back for the birds. The jays are the first to arrive. They carry
off the peanuts. Dan sends a Merry Christmas text. I reply
with the same message.

He texts, *What did you get from Dad?*

I reply, *Perfect Meatloaf Pan.*

He writes, *Real African Mango Weight Loss System.*

WTF? Are they pills? What about Allison-Jean?

Yes, pills. A RoboStir.

What's that?

It's like a whisk that stirs by itself.

Fuck, I type.

What time for dinner?

I reply, *5. We're having meatloaf instead of turkey.*

K, he writes, *Anything that needs stirring, we've got
covered.*

Smaller birds assemble at the bird feeder and peck at what's
left. They remind me of my children. Feisty and petite. Eager.
Other than the occasional squawk it is quiet outside. There
is no sign of the deer. The highway traffic is light. Wes slides
open the glass door.

"Open this now!" he hollers, holding a Clone Trooper.

"Excuse me? Is that any way to talk your mother?"

"I said please."

"No you didn't." I grab it from him. "Go get dressed."

"Why?"

"Because you're going to your Uncle Dan's for a bit."

"What for?"

"Because it's Christmas and that's what you do on Christmas. You play with your toys and you spend time with family and have dinner and stuff."

"Can I bring my Clone Trooper?"

"Yes, but hurry up and get dressed. Mommy has to start getting ready for dinner."

I drop the kids off at Dan's and spend the afternoon cooking a large bird and chopping vegetables. I accidentally drop two peeled potatoes in the garbage and call them assholes then I burn a piecrust and tell it to fuck off. My mother would not like this. She was calm in the kitchen and organized and did not curse. She kept her favourite recipes laminated and wore an apron. I didn't even wash my hands before I started prepping the meal.

After checking the progress of the turkey, I shower and dress. The tree still has nothing on top and I make a second attempt to find the Christmas decorations. The basement is cold. After checking a few Rubbermaid bins filled with manuals for small appliances, VHS tapes, and notes from university, I give up. I return upstairs, pull out the craft box, and begin fashioning an angel out of cardstock and pipe cleaners, saving the face for last. I take out a picture of my mother from a stack we'd sorted through before the funeral and use it as a reference. I work on the eyes several times but can't get them right. It's a terrible rendition, but I place her on the treetop anyway, just as Dan and Allison-Jean show up.

It takes them several trips to empty their van of food, gifts, their children and mine. Allison-Jean makes a beeline for the oven and pushes a dish of stuffing to the back. She is dressed up, as are her children. The baby looks like a Scottish golfer in her plaid beret and knit tights.

"Can I do anything?" she asks.

"I could use some help setting the table," I reply, putting
away the glue and scissors.

"What time's Dad coming?" Dan asks, pouring himself
a Guinness.

"Any minute."

He sips his beer then carries it cautiously to the living room.
Allison-Jean sets the table. She seems distressed by the mis-
matched plates and paper towels I put out instead of napkins.
The kids spread toys over the floor.

"Why don't you guys change?" I suggest to Wes and Joan.
Wes goes into his room and emerges in the same shirt but a
new pair of jogging pants.

"I meant into something nice."

"We don't have anything nice."

"Yes you do. Put that shirt on that buttons up the front."
He sighs, but leaves once again to get dressed. Joan comes out
in her bathing suit.

"No Joan. That is wrong." I pick her up and carry her back
to her room. "Let's put on a dress like your cousin Hannah."

She smiles in agreement and I lead her to her closet. She
chooses a summer dress. My father appears at her door in
time to help pull it over her head.

"How's my Joanie?" he says.

She gives him the thumbs-up and leads him down the hall.
He's wearing corduroy pants and a pit-stained turtleneck. He's
missed the belt loop at the back of his pants. The oven timer
goes off in the kitchen, and together Allison-Jean and I serve
up dinner. Dan gathers the kids to the table and feeds Emma
a bottle. My father does not offer to carve the turkey as he
does every Christmas. Instead he appears ready for a nap.

"Are you going to sleep, Dad?"

He perks up and sits upright in his chair. "No, no," he lies.

"Then, do you think you can do this?" I hold up the knife.

"Yes," he says rising to this feet. "Of course I can."

Allison-Jean and I take our seats. We catch each other glancing at the extra chair at the table. My mother's chair, in the same place it was during her birthday party.

Joan says, "Where Grandma?"

I point to the treetop and whisper, "Grandma's an angel, remember?"

"Where's Grandma?" Wes shouts from across the table.

"On the tree," I whisper, hoping my father can't hear our conversation from the kitchen where he's carving the bird.

"On the tree?" Wes appears confused.

Dan nervously pulls himself closer to the table.

"Well can we get her?" Wes asks.

Dan shakes his head. Nods towards my father in the kitchen.

"But she should be with us!" Wes argues.

My brother and I make eye contact and exchange gestures. Finally he gives in. "Whatever."

I go to the tree and pluck my mother off the top.

"Can I see?" Wes asks excitedly.

I hand him the angel. "I never knew Grandma was Asian."

"Wes, Grandma wasn't Asian."

"Yeah, but . . ."

"Mommy can't draw."

He shrugs his shoulders and hurries back to the table where he proudly places treetop Mom on her chair. Dad places a serving platter of turkey on the table. Dan quickly takes the visible dark meat, while Allison-Jean serves the kids. I remember the cranberry sauce is still in the fridge. I get up to retrieve it as my brother starts aggressively cutting his turkey.

"I think," my dad proposes, "we should each say something we miss about Janice."

Allison-Jean smiles weakly. Wes reaches for the treetop Grandma. I adjust his blue tissue crown from the cracker he snapped open earlier as he returns to his seat.

"I'll start," I offer. "I never thought I'd say this, but I miss the novelty earrings she wore at Christmas. And lipstick. Christmas was the only time she wore lipstick. There was something about that combination that made you realize just how much she loved Christmas."

My dad chuckles, "You're right," he agrees. "She used to get me to check her teeth for lipstick. They were always clean."

"I miss the way she sang to our kids," Allison-Jean says.

"Or hummed," I add.

"Or whistled," Dan says.

"Hummed, whistled. Didn't matter what it was, she could always get the kids to sleep," I say.

Dad pours gravy on his sweet potatoes.

"I like when Grandma gave us gum!" Wes shouts.

"Not so loud, Wes."

Dan swallows. "I miss her apple strudel. And how she put oranges in our stockings."

"That was me!" Dad says. There is a spot of gravy on his turtleneck.

"I liked her house," Hannah says quietly. Allison-Jean takes her daughter's hand and gives it a squeeze.

Liam says, "I liked how Grandma used to buy us a nut-cracker every Christmas."

I had forgotten about the nutcracker tradition. When it gets to Dad's turn, the adults anxiously await his answer. He wipes butter from his chin with the back of his hand. Manoeuvres his tongue behind his cheek like he's trying to remove food caught between his teeth. Then he crosses his arms, leans back in his chair, and says, "The thing I miss most about Janice is the way she folded the towels." And I start to laugh. Dan joins in.

"I'm serious!" My dad exclaims. "Your mother used to fold the towels perfectly. In thirds. They don't fit in the linen closet otherwise."

He takes his napkin from his lap.

"Watch kids." He pushes his plate forward and spreads the napkin in its place and says, "First you make sure all of the corners are flat."

Hannah and Liam observe carefully. My kids jam their cracker toys in their food. It alarms me that Liam is only six months older than Wes.

"Then you fold it in thirds. Yes, Hannah, just like that." Dad continues going through the steps.

"Pass me the turnip," Dan says.

When he is finished folding the napkin, Dad says, "There you go! Isn't that the perfect napkin? That is how she folded the towels." Dan and I start to laugh again and this time Dad joins in. The laughter spreads around the table like a junior high rumour until we realize Dad's crying. One by one the kids slip away from the table. Dan begins to well up and abruptly leaves the room. Allison-Jean throws her arms around my dad. Her big body envelops him like a sleeping bag.

"She would have loved that," she says affectionately. "It works with dishcloths too. You can fit more in the drawer that way."

He pats her arm with thanks and she exits, presumably to check on my brother.

I rise from the table and offer to make Dad some tea.

"I would like that," he replies. He sits alone with treetop Mom and waits while I go into the kitchen and fish a tea bag out of a Victorian Christmas tin. My brother joins me to deposit his empty beer stein. There is no space on the counter and he looks at me helplessly.

"Put it there," I gesture towards the stove.

He tucks the glass under his arm and carefully moves the stack of dirty dishes to make room. The challenge stresses him out because there is not enough space. When he attempts to push a pot out of the way, the glass slips from his armpit and falls. Gravy flies up and splashes his face.

"Help!" he cries.

"It's just gravy," I say, handing him a dishtowel.

He gags and says, "This is wet."

I turn my back and begin scraping plates into the garbage.

"Allison-Jean!" Dan calls.

Outside it starts to snow.

By the second week of January, most of Christmas has disappeared from view. The kids find the occasional piece of tinsel and floss with it, but most of the toys have been sawed out of their boxes and have been scattered around the house. Treetop Janice is packed away in a bin where she is likely to stay.

My father joins the local recreation centre and begins swimming in the mornings. Dan goes with him on occasion and they have breakfast together at a contemporary diner just outside of downtown. Cinnamon toast with fruit and hand-cut hash browns. I finish removing the roosters from the kitchen leaving a border of tobacco-yellow wallpaper glue behind. The new knobs I buy for the cupboards look wrong, like stilettos paired with track pants, and I give up halfway through the project.

At work I am temporarily assigned to sponsorship marketing. It is a break from proofing flyers and advertisements, but it means I have to attend events on behalf of the company starting with the Senior Winter Olympics. I want to slit my wrists.

I am filling the trunk of my car with biscuits and fruit trays in preparation for the opening ceremony when the daycare calls. It seems Wesley has become obsessed with death and has been asking his classmates how they want to die. Turtle Grove Daycare is not happy about this, and the administrator asks if Glen and I are available to discuss the issue.

I call him but he can't meet after work.

"Do you have any time now?" I ask. "Because I don't have to be at work until eleven."

I call Turtle Grove to let them know we are coming for 9:30 a.m. I arrive first but wait inside the car with my hands splayed in front of the vents. I can't get warm. Glen pulls up in a new SUV.

"Where's your car?" I ask as we head towards the doorway.

"It's not exactly a winter car." He tosses the long end of his scarf around his neck.

"So you have two cars now? Like a winter car and a summer car?"

"I have two cars," he affirms.

"Oh. I see. So what about spring? Fall? Cars for those seasons too?"

"No. It means I have two cars. Do you have a problem with that?"

"I don't even have a winter jacket."

"Then buy yourself a winter jacket."

He charges forward across the dry grass and doesn't hold the door open. Wes's teacher meets us outside the preschool room. The hallway smells like macaroni and bleach.

"Thanks for coming in," she says. Then she repeats some of the questions Wes has asked his classmates, including, "Would you rather die in an avalanche, be eaten by a bear, or get shot in a bucket?"

I make a mental note to ask Wes what it means to get shot in a bucket.

"The scenarios he offers are quite graphic and are disturbing to some of the children. I know you recently suffered a loss, but is there anything else going on we should be aware of?"

Glen and I share a dumbfounded exchange.

"I can't think of anything specific," I say. "I mean we certainly don't allow him to watch those types of shows on TV and he doesn't play video games and he isn't exposed to violence or anything." I look at Glen. "Can you think of anything?"

"No," he says shaking his head. "Occasionally I'll have the news on when he's in the room but if it's anything inappropriate I change the channel."

"Well perhaps he is still trying to cope with his grandmother's death." She lowers her voice to sound sensitive.

"Yes, maybe," I say.

"We'll talk to him," Glen assures Wes's teacher. "We'll sort it out."

"Please," she replies, shifting in her seat. She takes her glasses off and polishes them with her sweater then leaves to bring Wes from class.

I turn to Glen. "What does that mean, 'do you want to get shot in a bucket?'"

"It means he's four," Glen replies. "Most of what he says doesn't make sense."

"I know . . . it's just weird. I wonder what he meant."

"Please don't ask him."

I sigh. "I'm not going to ask him."

"This is the same kid who asked Santa for a peach turbine for Christmas."

"What the hell is a peach turbine?"

"Exactly."

"Okay, whatever," I say defensively, but Glen has already moved on.

He examines artwork on a bulletin board. Coloured turkeys, fire trucks, people that look like cucumbers with asterisks for hands. He is standing too close. Like he might be trying to sniff the drawings.

"Do you need glasses?" I ask.

"Pardon?" he says, looking at me over his shoulder.

"Glasses. Do you need glasses?"

"No, no. Just looking at the brush strokes."

"Right."

Wesley comes trudging through the door. "Daddy!" he yells. "Look at this!"

He hauls up his pants and shows off a bruise.

"How did you get that?" I ask, wondering if he got shot in a bucket.

"We were playing this game and there was this part where we had to like jump over this stick because it was like on fire and I smashed my knees on the floor like this." He demonstrates.

"Up off the floor," Glen orders. He bends down to refasten the Velcro on Wes's sneakers.

"Do you know why we are here, Wes?"

"To take me to McDonald's?"

"No," Glen says. "We are here because Mrs. Annie said you're asking your friends how they want to die."

"Yeah," he replies, puzzled.

I join the conversation. "Well that type of talk isn't appropriate for school. Do you understand?"

"Yeah." He picks at a staple on the bulletin board's alphabet border.

"Don't pick at that," Glen says. "Okay? And no more talk about death. Save those conversations for home. For Mom and Dad."

"Okay." He sighs. "Can we talk about it tonight?" He plays with his father's scarf.

Glen and I exchange frustrated glances.

"I won't be home tonight," Glen responds.

"But why?"

"I'm going to an art show after work."

"Are you taking the winter car or the summer car?" I ask.

Glen ignores me.

Wes asks Glen, "Is it your art show?

"Nope. It's a friend's."

"Does he make paintings?"

"It's a she and yes; she paints space landscapes."

"With aliens and stuff?"

"No, mostly just planets."

"Cool." Wes wrinkles his forehead. "Can I come too?"

"Next time," he says.

Mrs. Annie comes out of her office.

"Okay, Wes," I say, "it's time to go back to the classroom. Remember what we talked about?"

"Yes."

"What are you not going to do?"

"I'm not going to pick the staples off the bulletin board."

I throw my hands up in defeat and hurry off to the Senior Olympics.

The afternoon is long. I eat too much at the opening ceremonies and change into pajamas when I get home. I make Cream of Wheat for supper while the kids watch *Antiques Road Show* with peculiar interest. A cheerful bald man sits at one of the tables with a leather-bound dictionary. When the appraiser says it could fetch as much as eighty thousand dollars he nearly falls out of his chair. The amount flashes on the screen accompanied by the sound effect of a magic wand. Musical stardust. Wes mimics the sound. Uses his finger as a wand. I wonder what Perfect Meatloaf Pans are going for these days.

"Don't spill on the carpet," I caution, placing two glasses of apple juice on the coffee table. "Two hands, Joan."

I am out of glasses and pour myself juice in a rooster mug. On one side there is a red coq. On the other, in bold letters, Bonjour. It belonged to my mother. I took it home one night filled with chicken soup and never returned it. The only remaining rooster in the house.

Watching *Antiques Road Show* with the kids, I wonder what my dad will do with my mom's stuff. Her clothes and shoes, her Avon makeup. Most of it practical and none of it worth eighty thousand dollars.

After the last *Antiques* appraisal, I put the kids to bed and tidy up. The mug comes with me from room to room even after it is empty. A ceramic souvenir of my mother with an extra large handle. She would be so proud I watered the plants.

Wes gets out of bed and tiptoes down the hall.

"I can't sleep," he says.

I tell him to come to the kitchen where I'm loading the dishwasher.

"Why can't you sleep?"

He shrugs his shoulders. I pick him up by his armpits and hoist him onto the counter. He already has morning breath.

"Sometimes it's just hard to sleep," I say.

He nods and crosses his small feet at the ankles. His toenails are long and jagged, so I grab the clippers from the bathroom and cut them. I sweep the trimmings in my hand and dump them in the sink.

"Can I watch TV?"

"For a bit," I reply.

I wrap him in a blanket and carry him to the couch. He is both small and enormous. Little rib cage, big hair. My boy. I put on a kid's show and hand him the remote.

"I have to finish the laundry."

I go to my room to fold and divide clothes. Piles jut upwards from the floor like a cloth city. Three towers; I wonder if there will ever be a fourth. I fold the towels in thirds and notice an odour that resembles a tent city. Down on my knees I sniff each stack. Each one smells a little more like bum. I pull out a pair of Joan's one-piece pajamas. They are striped and covered in obese gingerbread men. I notice a bulge in the leg and unzip the jammies to investigate. I have washed and dried a shitty diaper. Lodged in the left foot, a piece of poop the size of a Timbit. Fuck. I throw the piles of folded clothes back in the laundry basket and kick it down the hall, leave it outside the closet-laundry-room with apartment-size machines.

Back in the living room, I recognize Alphonse Jr. on the TV: his big sneakers, the tattoos.

"Have you been watching this all along?" I ask, horrified.

"He got shot," Wes replies.

"Come on, it's bedtime."

With my hand on his upper back, we walk down the hall together.

"You shouldn't watch those shows. They're for grown-ups." I take a seat by his pillow.

"Why?"

"Because they're about death and they're sad. Death hurts people."

"But you said heaven was a happy place."

"Yes, I did say that, but death is still sad because you miss people when they're gone."

"Like Grandma?"

"Yeah, like Grandma."

"Is that why you're always sad?"

"I'm not always sad!"

I stare at my child and he looks back at me. Brown eyes wide and intense. His lightsaber glowing beside him.

"I am not always sad," I declare, smiling with effort. "I'm happy."

"Are you?" he asks. "Are you really happy?"

"Are you forty?" I reply.

He shakes his head and I smile again, this time sincerely. Though I'm also dumbfounded.

"No more shows about death, okay?"

He nods and I hold his head in my hands and kiss him hard on the cheek.

"I love you, okay?"

He nods again but I hesitate to leave. Caught up in the wonder of Wes. Of how I created such an odd mix of human. One both observant and clueless. Endearing and completely irritating. This is Glen and I. It's why we worked, it's why we failed. The lightsaber glows red beneath his sheet and makes a droning sound, like a bee.

"You know that show you just watched? They didn't happen to say who killed him . . . did they?"

"It was his friend," he says proudly. "His friend shot him."

"The guy with the green jacket?"

"Yeah, that guy!"

I knew it. I give him another kiss goodnight and close the door.

Saturday morning there's an article in the paper about a man charged for extorting his seventy-eight-year-old mother out of her life savings by threatening to kidnap her cat. A picture accompanies the article. The son wears jogging pants and looks like Chef Boyardee. My brother calls and I share the story with him but he tells me he's not interested.

I want to swear at him, but instead I just ask, "What's wrong with you?"

"Emma will not stop crying."

"I can hear that."

"So what do I do?"

"Have you tried to feed her? Is she hungry?"

"No she's not freaking hungry. I've fed her like six bottles."

"Well if you fed her six bottles, she's probably sick."

"Claudia!"

"Well? What does Allison-Jean think?"

"Allison-Jean isn't here."

"Try to burp her."

"And how do I burp her?"

"You don't know how to burp her? Didn't you ever have to burp Hannah or Liam?"

"Claudia, are you going to help me?"

I close the newspaper. "Put her on your shoulder and gently pat her back."

I pause, giving him time to follow direction.

"I'm putting you on speaker phone," Dan says.

"Are you okay? Where is Allison? Are you sick or something?"

"I just need her to stop crying."

"Who? Emma or Allison-Jean?"

"The baby!"

"Keep trying to burp her and call me back in ten minutes if it doesn't work. Where's Allison?"

He hangs up.

That was bizarre, I think, dialling my dad.

"Hi, honey," he answers cheerily. "I only have a minute here. I'm volunteering at the curling club this morning."

"Sure. Anything new?"

He hums for a minute and then replies, "Not that I can think of."

"Okay. Have you talked to Dan lately?"

"Not recently. He missed swimming this week because he was busy at work."

"Oh."

"Is everything okay?"

"Yeah, yeah. Just wondering if you talked to him. What are you doing at the curling club this morning?"

"We're fixing up the change rooms."

"Cool. Listen, I was thinking the other day about Mom's stuff. Maybe we should go through it sometime?"

"No," Dad chirps. "No, no, no."

"Okay, so *no?*"

"No. We don't need to do that."

"All right then, I just thought it might be good to start going through some of her stuff. Her clothes and things. You know? Her makeup, shoes. Maybe we could have a garage sale in the spring. Or we could donate some of it. Mom would like that."

"We can talk about that later. I have to get going because I have the key to the club."

"Okay."

I hang up.

An hour passes and I don't hear back from Dan. I assume he was able to settle the baby. The kids and I spend the morning lounging, and while they strip their beds and build forts in the living room, I think about my brother. The cowlicks in his hair, his fleshy wife. I'm embarrassed that he doesn't know how to burp his daughter. Glen was at least hands-on when Wes and Joan were babies. Took an hour to dress them, but he had the basics down.

The kids take turns crawling through the makeshift back door of the fort and shout unintelligible things at each other. Joan hits her head on the TV stand.

"Don't throw that!" I warn, seeing her wind up with the remote in her hand.

She hesitates. "Me go throw dis," she says, holding up the remote.

"Don't you dare."

She throws it. A clear pitch. It sails through the air and hits the wall. The batteries empty out and roll in opposite directions.

"Go to your room." I point.

She makes a beeline for the kitchen. I snare her midway, carry her under my arm, and put her on her bed.

"DO NOT THROW THINGS."

I close the door and hear the books empty off her shelf.

"Claudia?"

"Dan?" I head down the hall. "What are you doing here?"

"I need you to watch the kids for a bit," he says, setting the car seat on the floor. Hannah and Liam take off their Crocs.

"All of them?" I ask, staring at the baby.

"Yes, all of them," he replies irritably.

"Okay . . . why?"

"Because I need to go into work for a few hours."

"But it's a Saturday. Since when do you work on Saturdays?"

He turns and stares at me with his red eyes. He looks slightly deranged.

"Easy," I say. "What is wrong with you?"

"Hannah, Liam, take off your coats and go over there." He points to the fort in the living room. They do as they're told.

"Seriously, Dan. What's going on? Where's Allison-Jean?"

"Allison," he whispers, "is crazy."

"What do you mean?"

"She has post-partum depression."

"She does?" I ask, shocked. "Where is she?"

"At her mother's."

"Maybe she just needs a little break."

"It has lasted for weeks. We have an infant!" He gestures to Emma who has slithered halfway out of her unbuckled car seat. "I have missed a week of work!"

"You've had the kids on your own for the past week?"

"Yes!" He throws his hands up by the sides of his head, fingers crimped and full of tension.

"Don't yell at me! You could have asked for help earlier. When is she coming back?" I take a few steps down the hall towards the kitchen, and look in on the kids, playing in the living room. Hannah's hair is matted, unwashed. Is Liam wearing socks? These kids look like they could be mine.

"Hell if I know," he says, lingering in the hall, eyeing the baby in the car seat nervously. "She has a doctor's appointment for Monday. Can you just watch the kids for a couple of hours?"

"Yeah, yeah. Of course. But you should get some rest or something. Take a shower or brush your teeth. Are you hungry?" I look around the kitchen and go to the fruit bowl. "Here, take an apple."

"I'm fine," he says, waving it away.

I shrug and take a bite. "Did you bring a bag for them?"

"What do you mean?"

"Like a diaper bag with formula, bottles, that kind of stuff."

"I assumed you had bottles."

"Joan's almost three. I have a few sippy cups, but I don't have any bottles, and I definitely don't have any formula."

"Do you have milk?"

"Yes, I have milk, but you can't feed an infant skim milk."

"Why not?"

"Because you just don't! She's only a month old!"

"What about water, then?"

"Holy shit, Dan. I will have to go get some formula."

I pick the baby up from the car seat. She smells of artificial milk and feet. I allow my nose to adjust and fix her sloppy socks. She jams her fist in her mouth.

"Hi, baby," I say.

Dan returns to the door. "I'll be back in a few hours."

"Yeah, clean yourself up, will you?"

I am alone with five kids on a Saturday. I feel like a Duggar. It occurs to me that I can't even go to the grocery store because I don't have enough seats in the car. I dial my father but he has already left for the rink. He has not changed the voice-mail recording and it's my mother who informs me that no one is home. Her voice and the tiny body now settled in the crook of my arm throw me. I need to smoke something or eat a whole cake. Instead, I ram my feet into Hannah's fuchsia Crocs, peel a blanket off the top of the fort on my way through the living room, and swaddle it around the baby. I carry Emma out to the back deck. The cold shortens my breath. I adjust her to an upright position on my chest. My fingertips just fit between her shoulder blades. Wind blows her wispy hair into tall stalks that I smooth down. I kick up the barbecue cover, but the spare booster seat isn't underneath. Glen probably has it. I consider taking the double stroller but I remember the wheels are flat.

Back inside the house I call Cathy. "Can you come over for a bit?"

"You okay?"

"Dan dropped off his kids and forgot to bring formula. I need to run to the store."

"I'm at the shop this morning, but I can get out of here. Give me fifteen minutes."

She talks to someone in the background before hanging up. I can't make out what she says over the sounds of the garage. Clinking and whizzing. A robot dinner party.

When Cathy arrives in her coveralls and greasy hands, the kids are all playing in the fort with the TV blasting, while I'm wiping crusted formula off of Emma's face.

"Hey kids!" she yells from the front door.

Wes pokes his head out of the fort. "Cathy! Come in our fort!"

Cathy unties her work boots. "I just need to wash my hands."

"Thank you so much," I say, changing Emma from one hip to the other. "I won't be long."

She washes her hands in the kitchen sink with PEI red dirt soap she must have found under the sink; I forgot I even had that. "I'm in no rush," she says. She dries her hands on the back of her coveralls, while I strap the baby into her car seat. By the time I put the seat in the car without its base, Emma is asleep. I pause before closing the back door to observe. The downy hair on her ears that are small and perfectly round. Her lips pale and flutter-sucking. I stroke the top of her nose and shut the door.

I race to the baby section in the grocery store with the car seat weighing down my arm and banging against my thigh. There are ten thousand kinds of formula. Soy-based, kosher, lactose-free, ones with rice starch, ones that fight acne, ones that play music. I buy the one with the happiest looking baby on the label, some bottles, and a package of diapers. The lines are long and I tap my foot impatiently.

On my way to the car my phone rings but I can't get to it. I put Emma in the back and see it was Dan. I go to call him back but the bag with the formula in it splits and cans of Happy Baby roll underneath the car. I kneel down and collect them and toss them onto the front seat. The Happy Babies are assholes but I still let them ride shotgun.

When I get home, Dan's car is in the driveway. What the heck? Inside, he and Cathy are talking in the kitchen.

"What are you doing back so soon?"

"I forgot my proxy card at home. I couldn't get into my office."

"I just spent like fifty bucks on this stuff," I say plunking the diapers and formula on the counter.

He bends down as Emma starts to whimper in her car seat, her eyes still closed, and mumbles, "Sorry."

"You should change her," I suggest. He stares up at me. "Give her to me." He takes her out of her car seat and passes her to me. "Let's go change your bum," I say grabbing the diapers from the counter.

Cathy excuses herself from the kitchen. "I told them I'd go in the fort," she says.

I lay Emma in the hall, pull off her leggings, and watch Cathy in the living room open the fort's side flap and crawl in. Hannah and Liam go around the back and attempt to do the same but there's not enough room. Liam's legs and Hannah's head stick outside, her ponytail draped behind her like spilt milk. They look dejected. They want their mom. The fort begins to move. The roof slips off exposing Cathy attempting to stand.

"Cathy!" Hannah calls out, "You can't stand up."

"Now we have to start all over," Wes whines.

I look at my brother standing in the kitchen. Hair unkempt, a week's worth of stubble, shirt un-tucked, no belt. "Go home," I tell him. "I'll keep them for the night."

"Even Emma?"

"Get some rest, Dan. I got her."

He looks completely pathetic and like he might try to hug me, but instead he gives me fifty bucks for the diapers and formula and kisses each of his kids goodbye.

The kids play musical beds moving from one room to the next. They swap sleeping bags and positions. No one wins. Emma sleeps beside me in my own bed. A strange and wriggly bedfellow.

In the morning I do a head count. Joan turns on *The Littlest Hobo*. All the kids watch, mesmerized, from the table where I dispense four bowls of cereal like it's summer camp.

Dan, looking refreshed, arrives to pick them up just before 10:00 a.m. He brings me a 7-Eleven coffee that smells nutty. I take a sip from my coffee, standing in the driveway, watching my brother pack his kids in the car. He takes the steering wheel and adjusts things on the dash the way he did in the makeshift cars we drove as kids. Opening vents, turning dials, depressing buttons. Cars made from empty appliance boxes. The broken picnic table. Two stools in the sandbox. He backs down the driveway and disappears up the street.

Joan stands an inch from the TV screen, fascinated by a little girl in a wheelchair ministering to a man in blue pajamas. He is also in a wheelchair, newly paralyzed. Quadriplegic and in denial. Wes is less enthusiastic. He pays little attention until the man starts hollering and the dog mysteriously arrives at the hospital.

Joan attacks the carpet with my round hairbrush.

"Don't use that on the carpet," I say. "That's dirty."

She tells me to sit down so she can brush my hair. A male nurse enters the hospital room and tells the patient he's going swimming. The patient hollers, "No!"

"Is he going to kill him?" Wes asks.

I try to explain the story as the nurse swoops up the bald

man, places him in the chair, and wheels him to the pool where
the girl waits in a bathing cap that is red like my mother's.

"Is *she* going to kill him?" Wes asks, hopeful.

"No. No one is going to kill him. That hurts, Joan." I
massage the top of my head where my hair has been yanked.
"Brush it gently."

She takes offense, brushes harder, and then says, "It just
an accident."

By the end of his swim, the man has accepted his disability.
Joan manages to get this and stops brushing to clap.

"What's happening now?" Wes asks as the man leaves the
hospital in his wheelchair.

"He's off-roading," I reply.

"Where he going?" Joan asks.

"I don't know, you'll have to watch."

He comes upon his child companion who has somehow
managed to fall out of her own wheelchair and down an
embankment. She looks like I did as a child. Long braids,
plaid dress, dirty face.

"Is she dead?" Wes asks.

I tell him she's probably only unconscious and go on to
explain what that is. "It's sort of like she's sleeping."

"Then where's her tent?"

"She's not camping. She fell out of her chair."

In a courageous effort, the man in the blue pajamas throws
himself out of his chair and hurls himself down the hill.
Seconds later the dog arrives and runs for help.

"Dog!" Joan exclaims.

"Yes. He's going to save them."

Joan comes around in front of me. Picks up a stray peanut
off the floor and eats it. I pat the top of my head. The brush is
attached to it. Sitting an inch off my scalp. I tug at it gently.

"Wes, see if you can take this brush out of my hair."

"Where did that dog go?"

"Wes, try and unravel this."

He stares at me blankly. "Is he going to get a doctor?"

"Yes, now see if you can get this out."

My face starts to get hot.

"How does the dog know where to find a doctor?"

"Because he's magic."

In the bathroom I stare at the bird's nest on the top of my head. I try and manoeuvre the brush forward so I might be able to unravel some of the hair but it's a matted mess. I hear screaming from the living room and return to find Joan straddling Wes.

"She bit me!"

"Joan! Get off your brother right now." The brush sways a bit as I stomp across the room. Joan wraps her arms tight around Wes's neck and he flails his legs and tries to buck her off. I hoist her up by the waist but she bends backwards and jabs her finger into my eye. I put her on the couch and cover my face. The theme song from *The Littlest Hobo* plays.

"I didn't see how they got saved!" Wes cries.

Joan escapes down the hall, her wide feet flapping loudly against the laminate. I can't open my eye. I am now a Cyclops sporting a bouffant. A steady stream of tears trickles down my face from the poked eye. I order Wes to get my phone.

"Who are you calling?" Wes whines.

"I need to find a babysitter."

"Can you tell Cathy?" Joan asks.

"Go back to your room," I yell. "Look at Mommy's eye and look at the bite mark on your brother's cheek."

Wes picks up my phone. "Can I play Angry Birds?"

"No." I take the phone from Wes and call my father. It's nearly an hour before he's at my house. When he arrives, he braces himself against the wall and pulls off his loafers with a grunt. He's not wearing socks. I don't look at his toenails in case they are too long, like his hair.

My dad stands facing me. "Can you open it?" he asks, tilting my chin up to examine my eye.

"No," I wince. "It stings."

He looks at the brush, puzzled. "Yep, I think you should go in."

I sigh and gather my belongings. "Be good for Grandpa," I caution.

I return home from the emergency room well after the kids' bedtime with a maxi pad taped over my left eye and the brush still attached to my head, smelling like hospital. I pull off my sweatshirt and dump it in the hall. My father sits at the kitchen table, hovering over a bowl, milk dripping from his chin.

"Were the kids okay?" I ask, peeking into Wes's room.

"They're in your room. They wanted to sleep in your bed." Dad points at the brush. "They couldn't get that out?"

"Unfortunately, no. They remove bullets, not brushes." I sit beside him.

He reaches over and gives the brush a little tug. "Where's your mother when you need her? I'll give it a try."

He begins pulling and unraveling my hair from the brush, a few strands at a time. I bite my lip. It reminds me of when my mom French-braided my hair. For such a mild-mannered woman she was an aggressive braider.

"Ouch!"

"Sorry," my father apologizes, "it's almost out."

I cringe under the strain, look down at the floor. My father's toenails are impossibly long. Yellowed claws. He hands me the brush.

"Dad, you need to cut your toenails." He studies his feet

while I massage the top of my head feeling for bald spots. "When's the last time you cut them?"

He shrugs. "I don't know where your mom keeps the clippers."

When I go to the bathroom to retrieve the steel clippers from under the sink, I glance in the mirror and see the small goatee on top of my head.

Returning to the kitchen, I hand the clippers to my father. "Here, you need to cut them."

He rolls up his pant legs and begins snapping off his nails with the clippers held backwards.

"Hold them the other way."

He flips them over and works on his big toe, cutting the nail into the shape of an arrowhead and proceeding to the next.

"Whoa, back up. You need to fix that." I can't tell if it's inexperience or age. His eyes indicate a bit of both. "Here, let me do it."

I pull up a chair across from him and rest his foot on the edge between my legs. His foot is surprisingly soft. There's a sprig of grey curls on his big toe. I trim the big toenail first then move on to the others, methodical in my execution. My father pays close attention. I hand him the clippers.

"You have to cut them regularly. Okay?"

He nods. "Yes, I will do that."

He rises from his chair, and pats me, once, on the shoulder. Then he heads into the entryway, retrieves his coat from the floor, slips into his unlaced loafers, and heads out the front door.

"Love you," I call after him. "Call me when you get home so I know you got there safe."

After the front door closes behind him, I go straight to the sink and wash my hands. When I look down I still see my father's feet. His thick nails, crooked metatarsi, raised veins.

I gag and rinse. My left eye itches beneath the patch and I attempt to rub it with my shoulder. My mother told me that Jesus washed his disciples' feet. I wonder if he cut their nails too. I think Mom did both for my dad.

After forty minutes, I phone Dad. "You were supposed to call when you got home."

"Sorry. Let me turn down the music."

"I wanted to know you got home safe."

"Yes, yes." He yawns. "I'm so tired."

"Why don't you go to bed?"

"What time is it?"

I look at the clock. "Twenty after ten. When do you normally go to bed?"

"I often fall asleep in my chair."

"That's probably not good for your neck."

"You're probably right. Your mother would make sure I came to bed before then."

"From now on you should go when you're tired. You need a good night's sleep."

He yawns again. "I should have paid more attention. I didn't know she was going to die."

"I know."

"Now I don't know when I'm supposed to go to bed or how often I should see the dentist. And the mail. What of it do I toss? What am I allowed to keep?"

"Toss the flyers."

"But your mom loved the flyers."

"Then keep them until the next ones come."

We both say nothing for a moment, but stay on the line. I hear him adjust his weight in his chair. The muffled warble of old springs.

"Dad," I say, "it's time to go to bed."

Glen comes for dinner Wednesday night before taking Wes to his Beavers' meeting. I make spaghetti and garlic bread. Joan's face turns orange from the sauce.

"So what did you say happened?"

"Joan jabbed me with her nail."

He leans over the table and examines my eye. He's wearing cologne.

"Is it better? It looks better."

"I took the patch off yesterday. Listen, I need you to take the kids for a few days in April during the workweek. Can you do that?"

"I have to check my schedule. Why?"

"Because I have to go to Calgary for training."

Joan eats with her hands. "Daddy, you know dis movie called Wonka —"

I interrupt, "Wipe your chin."

"I do know *Willy Wonka*," Glen says.

"So can you?" I ask him.

"Probably. You have to go all the way to Calgary for training?"

"The regional one was in October."

"When your mom . . ."

"Died!" Wes finishes.

We both look at our son.

"Yes. When Grandma died."

Glen gives me a sympathetic look and wipes Joan's face with a napkin.

"Dere's dis boy. He Charlie," she says.

"I know," Glen responds, taking another piece of garlic bread. "You must like that movie."

Joan says, "Me love it," and attempts to explain the plot. "He has to find go-den ticket and dere's dis big boo-berry."

"I used to watch it when I was young," I tell her.

She looks at me temporarily then resumes gazing at her father.

I get up and clear the table and put the Parmesan cheese in the freezer by accident, noticing that half a dozen Freezies I bought in the summer have leaked and re-frozen to the side door.

I retrieve Wes's Beavers uniform from the back of his door. The pants look too short. The necktie is cartoonish and makes me think of Willy Wonka. Specifically the ugly kid who plays Charlie. There is something mildly gross about him and his house with all the old people lying in their beds with rickets or dysentery or whatever it is that has made them bedridden. And Grandpa Joe with his dirty Einstein hair, and the way he dances when they find the golden ticket. I want to punch him in the throat.

"Wes, come get your uniform on," I call.

"I can help him with it," Glen volunteers, and both he and Wes join me in Wes's bedroom.

"Arms up," he says, pulling Wes's shirt over his head. A lump of ground beef plops to the floor. Glen picks it up with a Kleenex. I gather dirty clothes strewn about Wes's room and throw them in a laundry basket. My knees make an audible crack when I bend down.

"You should get going," I suggest to Glen.

He checks his watch and hurries Wes along.

When I open the front door for them, the cold enters. I shiver and kiss Wes on both cheeks and tell him to listen to his Beavers' leader.

"Have fun."

Back in the kitchen, I clear the table, stepping over the railway tracks Joan has assembled on the floor. She strings together a row of Thomas trains and pushes them along quietly. She drives over my foot with Diesel 10.

"What do you want to do?" I ask her.

She looks up at me with her dark grey eyes and her pink cheeks and then makes a pig nose.

"Charming," I say. "Shall we have a bath?"

She nods.

I fill the bath, strip her down, and plunk her in the tub.

"Watch dis," she says, squirting a whale bath toy.

I do watch. I also sit on the side of the tub and read texts from Cathy. She is stuck at the shop. One of her mechanics called in sick. She asks about the kids.

I text, *Kids are good. Wes is at Beavers with Glen. Just bathing Joan.*

"Look Mommy," Joan says.

I tell her "just a second," and check my email.

"Mommy!" She tugs on my arm.

"Don't, Joan. You're getting water on my phone."

Cathy replies, *Sportchek has buy one get fifty percent off right now on sneakers.*

I begin to text her back but Joan starts choking on bath water she is drinking from a plastic tugboat. I gently thump the top of her back. "Don't drink that."

I use the last of the watermelon shampoo to wash my girl's hair and remember when she had none. It seems like yesterday she was hairless and curious and blithe and I was captivated by her blitheness. Now she bites people and jabs eyeballs with her fingernail and on a bad day I've called her an asshole in my head. I really think that's when being a parent is most difficult. Not the sleepless nights or the fits at the grocery store or the brushes stuck to your head, but when your child does something an asshole would and you actually think it. *Asshole.* You think it and you feel it and then you feel sick, like you've just seen a cat get hit by a car, because when you first held her in the hospital and she weighed five pounds and she gazed in your eyes and you fell in love, did you ever imagine you would one day think she was an asshole?

Kneeling, I wrap Joan tight in her towel. The blue one, because it's her favourite colour. The bath mat is damp. I hug her and rock her in the steamy bathroom, feeling guilty, and notice my toothbrush has fallen beside the toilet.

Winter bows out with little pomp, no grand finale. I only notice its absence when I pull into Sobeys and the snowplow mountain is missing. Left in its place is a pile of displaced gravel my children insist on rifling through. It is spring. My mother has been gone for five months, but there are distractions: fat lilac bushes, third birthdays, and a new toaster oven. And behind the backyard porch light, a nest of baby robins. Heavy-headed, helpless, hungry. We watched them hatch from the back door. Wes on a stool, Joan on my shoulders.

Our first family gathering since Christmas is the last Sunday in March. It's also my first look at my sister-in-law since her breakdown. When we arrive Allison-Jean opens the door before I have a chance to knock. She looks skinnier than normal, but she's still big. She holds the door open and helps my kids remove their shoes.

"Hannah and Liam are downstairs," she says. "We just put on *Toy Story 3*."

"*Toy Story 3* is for babies," Wes whines.

"You're four, Wes. It's fine," I tell him. I hang my coat on one of the guest hooks beside the hall closet. "Go down and play. Allison, you look great."

"Uh, thanks," she mumbles on her way to the kitchen.

"Claudia!" my dad calls from the living room. He's wearing a white terry cloth headband with a navy stripe.

"Hey, Dad. Are you wearing a headband?"

"We're playing tennis, aren't we?" he says with his arms outstretched.

I hug him and look at the remote wrapped around his wrist. "Wii tennis."

"Exactly." He adjusts the headband. "Keeps the hair out of my eyes."

My brother doesn't greet me. He fiddles with one of several remotes until the Wii screen appears.

"Who's ready to play?"

Allison-Jean returns from the kitchen with a bowl of Bits & Bites, which I decline because they have Shreddies in them. Cereal should be doused with brown sugar. Not salt pellets and spicy dust.

"You're first, Dad," Dan says, passing him a Wii remote. "We're bowling."

"I thought we were playing tennis?" Dad says, adjusting the remote around his wrist. But he quickly switches gears, circles his arms as though warming up, and then says, "Here we go," and takes his turn. He waits in anticipation then yells, "Sttrrriiike!" the way an umpire would call it. He hands me the remote and claps for himself. "Beat that, Claud," he adds.

I bowl a spare and pass my remote to Allison-Jean. Looking around the room, I observe that her house does not look like it has been through post-partum depression. The books are still shelved by colour and it smells like Michaels art store.

Allison-Jean stares at the round avatar ready to bowl on the screen. "Is that supposed to be me?" she asks. "Because I look enormous."

"No," Dan says. "You don't have a Mii."

"How come?"

"Because you have to go in and make one."

"What do all those numbers and letters mean?"

"That's your name."

"How come your character has a name and mine is X7Y-PU769?"

Dan sighs. "The kids made that one."

"I want my own Mii."

Dan looks irritated. "But you never play."

"Just make her a Mii," I say.

He gets impatient but gives in. Goes to the home screen and selects new Mii. He picks features hastily. "What colour shirt do you want?"

Allison-Jean says, "Purple." Her Mii's chest rises and falls as though it is breathing.

"Is that good?" Dan asks.

"No, that's not good. That looks like Chaz Bono!"

"It does not."

"Who's Chaz Bono?" Dad asks.

Dan replies, "The lead singer of U2."

"That's *Bono*, you idiot. Chaz Bono is Sonny and Cher's daughter," Allison-Jean glares at Dan with her eyes all big and her neck extended.

Trying to be helpful, I say, "It does not look like Chaz Bono. For one thing, Chaz Bono is now a man and secondly . . ." I trail off, unable to think of a second thing. I come up with, "He doesn't bowl."

"He doesn't bowl? Thanks, Claud," Dan says. "That's helpful."

Allison-Jean grabs the Wii remote and tells Dan, "Shut up." She lengthens her Mii's hair and makes her thinner. She flicks her wrist to the side and begins entering the letters of her name. The clicking sound when she makes a selection reminds me of chattering teeth. Allison-Jean spells Allison-Jon.

"I hate this," she says.

Down the hall Emma begins to cry. Allison-Jean gives the remote to Dan and heads off to get her.

"I signed up to play in a bonspiel in April," Dad announces.

"Nice!" I reply.

Dan focuses on his shot, altering his angle ten degrees left. He steps back from the TV and releases his Wii ball. It only knocks down one pin.

"No fair!" he hollers, examining the remote for the cause of his extreme curveball. He takes a second shot and the ball goes in the gutter. He stomps his foot.

"Dan!" Allison-Jean says, placing Emma in her ExerSaucer.

"What? This is ridiculous."

"Remember when you missed that penalty shot at soccer provincials and you blamed it on the ref?" I ask.

Allison-Jean holds up a beer to me from the kitchen. I nod and say, "Please."

"I did not blame it on the ref."

"Oh, I remember that," Dad says, proud of himself. "You said he was in your way."

Dan rolls his eyes. "He *was* in my way. He was too close."

"He was nowhere near you, son," Dad replies, strapping the Wii remote back on his wrist. "Your mother had to ride home in the back seat to console you."

"Didn't you hit something too?" I add, twisting the cap off my beer. "Like a sign or something?"

"I did not," Dan says, spit flying.

"No, it was the ball bag," Dad says. "You came off the field and kicked the ball bag."

"Yes!" I say, jumping to my feet. "And all the balls rolled out and your coach made you pick them up."

Dad bowls another strike and hands the remote back to

my brother. "Let's go, Danny," he says, clapping his hands with encouragement.

"I'm not playing!" Dan shouts, tossing the remote onto the couch.

"Dan," Allison says, "it's a game. Relax."

"Well I'm not playing!" He picks up his beer and downs half the bottle. Foam tumbles out of the top and decorates his upper lip.

We're all silent for a moment and look at the TV. And there in the back of the Wii bowling alley, behind the score table, is our Mii mother. She says nothing. Only wobbles slightly, the way a cell might under a microscope, and waits for Dad to bowl.

"That's weird," I say.

"It's creepy is what it is," Dan says. "Delete her profile."

"We can't just *delete* her profile," I argue.

"Yes, we can."

Dad just continues to stare at his Mii wife. "It really does look like her. Except for the eyebrows. The eyebrows are too high up."

"Oh, you can fix that," I tell him.

"We're not going to fix anything," Dan cuts in. "I'm deleting her."

"Isn't that Glen?" Allison-Jean says. "Behind your mom, in the orange shirt?"

"No," I reply, "that's ZPF678VG. Glen's on the other side with the goatee." If anything, it's Mii Glen who looks like Chaz Bono.

I take the remote and lower Mii mom's eyebrows.

"Is that it?" I check with Dad.

"Yeah," he says. "It really looks like her." He nods his head with satisfaction. I save and quit.

"That's fine," Dan says, crossing his arms. "But it's my Wii and I'll just delete her when you leave."

"Come on, Dan. It's just like real life. Mom showing up at all of your games."

"I'm not remembering my mother in the form of a digital marionette."

"Marionettes have strings."

"What the heck ever," he says, the heck part blurred by a burp. "A doll then. I don't want to remember her as a little digital doll that sometimes has no legs."

"Yeah, why is it that some of the Miis don't have legs?" Dad asks. He pulls up his pant leg to scratch and reveals a gargantuan white sport sock.

I say, "I think it's only the stranger Miis who don't have any legs."

Allison-Jean asks, "Whose turn is it?"

I strap the Wii remote to my wrist and tighten the strap. "Tennis, anyone?"

A week later, I drop the kids off at Glen's for the morning and head to Canadian Tire to return a planter. The store is almost empty. I hoist the planter up on the customer service desk and tell the clerk I need to return it. She examines it and asks if there's anything wrong with it. I show her the crack on the bottom and hand her my receipt. My father enters the store and has trouble manipulating the turnstile.

"Dad!" I yell.

My father looks around but doesn't see me, and he heads towards the paint department. The clerk hands me back my receipt, which is covered in black marks to remind me I'm going to hell for making a return. After she's made the refund on my card, I return my Visa to my wallet and head after my dad, who is squatting in an aisle.

"Dad," I say. He turns and I help pull him up to standing. "What are you doing here?"

"I'm looking for stain," he says, "but I forgot to write down the colour."

"Stain for what?"

"Oh, I'm refinishing this old chair for a lady I curl with."

"You don't know how to refinish things."

"Yes, I do," he says. "I learned it off the Internet."

"Are you sure?"

"Yes. Now if I could only remember what colour . . ."

"I thought you'd be at the rink practicing for your big debut in a couple weeks."

"Going to practice tomorrow," he replies proudly. "Are you
and the kids going to come to the bonspiel?"

"We'll try." I try to imagine myself in the rink surrounded
by droves of soft-bodied happy people who like to organize
potlucks and wear fancy tracksuits. "You didn't happen to
bring the chair with you?" I ask, changing the subject.

"Yes, actually. It's in the trunk. Do you want to see it?"

I follow my dad out of the store, as the clerk leans her back
against the counter, her ankles crossed, watching us leave. In
the parking lot my dad opens the trunk and shows me an old
chair with an intricate back and caned seat.

"What colour would you say that is?"

"No idea. Looks like dark cherry or something."

Dad pats the pockets of his jacket. "I should have brought
my glasses," he says. "I'll have to do this tomorrow." He covers
the chair with a brown blanket and closes the trunk.

"Don't ruin that," I warn. "It looks worth something."

My dad seems surprised by my concern. He looks old in
the sunlight, his chin taking on the appearance of a raisin.
He reaches inside his collar and scratches his chest. I wait for
him to finish and beckon him towards me.

"Come here, Dad."

I hug him long and hard. Rest my head against his chest.
After several seconds he pulls away and smiles.

"I should go," I say, though I can't remember where I parked
my car and need to survey the lot. "I have some errands to do
for my trip Thursday."

"Where are you going?" he asks.

"Just Calgary for a few days. For work."

"Well that should be fun," he says.

"Nah, it's training. I'll call you with my hotel information before I go."

"I should get home too. These damn bedbugs are killing me. I've got to find some Raid or something."

"What?" I say, backing up. "Bedbugs?"

"Pretty sure. Got their damn bites all over me. Say, what's that pink stuff your mom used to rub on you kids? Begins with a 'c.' You know, that lotion?"

He snaps his fingers a couple of times. Long enough for me to wave goodbye, spot my car, and head over to it. I sit in my car for a few minutes. When I'm sure my dad's driven off, I go back into the store and empty a can of Raid all over my body.

I immediately tell Dan about Dad's bedbugs and that he has to call an exterminator, and then I call two different pharmacists and inquire about a morning-after pill for having unprotected hugging with a bedbug carrier. There is no such pill, so I take my third shower in less than twelve hours. My skin is raw from the scrubbing.

Monday morning, I go outside and tie off the garbage bag of clothes I burned the day before. The kids mill about the house in their pajamas.

"Do we have to go to school today?" Wes asks when I come back inside.

"Yes, but you're going to be late."

"How come?"

"Because we're running late."

Joan asks, "Because Grandpa has bugs?"

I reply, "Yes" and immediately regret it because she will spread the word.

"Wes, go put your clothes on."

For no apparent reason, other than being four, Wes drops to the ground and crawls to the bedroom with his tongue hanging out.

"That's nice, Wes," I comment.

Joan bobs for Rice Krispies at the table. Milk drips from her face.

"Are you almost finished?"

She replies by pulling on the skin below her eyes.

I say, "Does that mean you're done?"

She excuses herself, goes to the living room, turns on the TV, and stands an inch from it.

It takes me a second to realize I'm scratching my back and I think of the bedbugs and my blood pressure goes up. I go to the bathroom and fold the mirrors around my body to look for bites but don't see any. Wes appears at the door with a helicopter.

"Are we going yet?"

"Five minutes," I say.

He spins the blades.

It takes another fifteen minutes before we're actually pulling out of the driveway. I put on a kids' CD and a happy person sings *Who built the ark?* and some happy kids reply *Noah! Noah!* Joan kicks her feet to the music and in my head I sing *Who brought the bugs? Father! Father!* and shiver.

Dan finally calls me back to say he can't get an exterminator into Dad's until the weekend.

"That's not good enough!" I say. "Call them back."

"You call them. Why is it my job anyway? Why can't Dad call his own exterminator?"

"It's your job to take care of bug things," I assert, pulling into the parking lot of Turtle Grove.

I hang up the phone and walk the kids into daycare where they hang their raincoats on their respective hooks and the school's director comes out of her office and greets them, and as they toddle off into the classroom, Wes sings "Who built the ark?" And Joan replies, "No one! No one!"

Glen agrees to pick up the kids from school Wednesday so I can work late.

He emails, *Why don't you just come for supper and I'll take the kids tonight? That way you don't have to drop them off tomorrow.*

I email back, *That would be great.*

I spend hours sorting through sponsorship requests from ball teams and animal shelters. In lieu of funding I offer ham sandwiches and store brand juice. Saying no depresses me. I print off my boarding pass and training schedule before shutting down and chatting with my assistant. I can't help but notice she looks pregnant. She catches me staring at her belly but says nothing.

"If the Legion calls, tell them I've approved their request and a letter is on the way."

She makes note of my instruction on a yellow pad, then sticks the pen behind her ear. "Have fun," she says, in reference to my trip.

"I'll try," I reply sarcastically.

I hurry out of the office feeling nauseous from work. Photocopies and light bulbs and the glass bowl of unwrapped spearmints in reception. I stop at home to finish packing before going to Glen's for dinner. When I arrive they have already eaten.

"Yours is in the oven," he says.

"Thanks."

"Mommy!" Wes calls enthusiastically from the hall. "Joan pooped on the toilet!"

I look at Glen for confirmation.

"True story," he says.

I find my girl with a colouring book on the kitchen floor and congratulate her. She elbows me out of the way and continues her work. I give her a dirty look she doesn't see and go to the table. Glen joins me out of courtesy. He's made salmon.

"This is good," I say.

"You sound surprised."

"Didn't mean to."

We talk casually. About work, his art, my dad. I notice my painting *In Contempt* is no longer on the wall behind him. I want to inquire about its whereabouts but am distracted. There is something different about Glen I can't pinpoint. It's not the shirt I've never seen before or the dill sauce he's put on the salmon. It's his demeanour. His contentedness. I see it in his arms, relaxed on the table, and in his eyes. And I see it everywhere else too. His clean countertops. The rapid thumping of George's tail against the floor.

"Claudia?" he asks.

"What?"

"I asked if you're okay?"

"Yes." I apologize, "Sorry. I have a bit of a headache."

"Why don't you go lie down?"

Wes calls an *American Idol* contestant an idiot in the next room.

"No, I should go home."

I fork the remainder of my spinach into my mouth.

"You sure?"

"Maybe for a few minutes."

I go off to Glen's room feeling equal parts fatigued and

out of sorts. I keep the lights off and the door ajar. His pillow does not smell like head the way it did when we lived together. It smells like grass. I drift off as he's telling the kids to brush their teeth.

When I wake up it is just after nine and I come to the questionable but likely conclusion that I've had an orgasm in my sleep. It leaves me confused and feeling a bit violated because I remember nothing about my dream other than trying to pass off a box of Band-Aids as a meat casserole.

Glen pops his head in the door. "You up?"

"Yeah."

"The kids are both asleep," he says.

"Oh."

I sit up in his bed and he continues to stand at the door, his hand still on the knob. I ponder the orgasm. Think about all the times I had to try really hard to make it happen awake and feel both fascinated and cheated.

"Are you okay?"

"I'll get out of your bed," I say, folding back the covers.

"No rush," he says. "Jays are on TV. Eleventh inning."

I go to the fridge and pour a glass of water, then nearly choke on the temperature.

"Don't forget Wes has a Beavers thing tomorrow night."

"Got it written down," Glen says in the other room. I notice that he does. It's on the fridge calendar.

I thank him for dinner and go to the kids' room.

"I'm proud of you," I whisper into Joan's ear. She stirs but stays asleep. I then climb the ladder to the upper bunk. "Bye Wes." I knock my shin on the way back down.

Outside the night air is cool and gives me a chill. I should've done up my jacket. I should've stopped eating when I was full. I should've known he'd found someone new.

I go from work to the airport. My flight to Calgary is delayed and I walk around the Halifax airport. It's too big to have character like an island airport and too small to get lost in the crowd. Everyone sits and stares at each other. A boy uses a box of lobster packed for travel as a seat. Seniors in blue tartan wander around ready to show off their Nova Scotian friendliness. My Kobo isn't charged.

It's another hour before we finally board, and after we do, the flight's not much better than the airport. The plane bounces around and they cancel the first drink service and neglect to pass out the little snacks normally fed to parrots. I stare out the window at nothingness and wonder where my mom was sitting before she died. Impossible. It's not even the same airline, but I touch everything around me just in case. Press my cheek against the window.

My shoe slips off my foot and I nearly have a panic attack trying to retrieve it. The seats are too close. By the time I manage to get it back on my foot, sweat is dripping down my chest.

"Can I get you a drink?"

A male flight attendant leans into the seat. I order a ginger ale. He hands me a package of cranberry citrus cookies that taste like cranberries and citrus and nothing like cookies.

"These are gross," I say to my neighbour, holding up the empty wrapper. He nods and goes back to reading an article on Mitt Romney, which I periodically attempt to read over his shoulder. I drink my orange juice too fast. Practically shoot it because I can't move or do anything as long as my tray table is down and any second now the flight attendant will want to collect my cup even though he just handed it over. I put it in the seat pocket and doze off.

On our way to Calgary, we divert to Toronto for a medical emergency. A woman in the rear of the plane is in labour. She breathes and snorts like a mechanical horse. Paramedics meet the plane. The flight attendant and a passenger guide her down the aisle and send her down the stairs and I wonder if it would have been easier if they'd inflated the giant yellow slide and rolled her down. I watch from my window as she is loaded into the back of the ambulance, her youthful face twisted, her pants wet. I start to get restless in my seat. Wish the flight attendant would escort me off too. Help me down the stairs and into a waiting suv full of Swiss Chalet fries and the flaming cheese they serve in Greek restaurants. Another flight attendant opens one of the overhead compartments and pulls out a large charcoal-coloured carry-on bag she then delivers to the ambulance. The captain comes on a few minutes later, unnecessarily explains the reason for our landing in Toronto, and says we will be back in the air shortly. First the pregnant woman's suitcase needs to be removed. In the meantime the ambulance takes off. It looks like a toy beside the planes. The luggage, I presume, will be held for the woman in the airport or perhaps delivered to the hospital. I watch below as the guy loads a black suitcase onto a waiting luggage trolley. It has a green tag and an orange bandana tied to the handle and if you look really closely you can see where Joan rubbed my deodorant across the zipper. The door closes, the flight attendant prepares for take-off, the plane begins to taxi, and I go to yell "stop" but it comes out like a dull "uhh" the way it does in dreams where you're being chased and you have no voice.

I think about pressing the call button, but the flight attendant has already fastened his seat belt and he might get mad or play the flute or something. Somewhere over Manitoba I realize it's too late to do anything but dig through my purse for a distraction. I find a small juice box left over from the Senior Olympics in the side pocket of my bag. I'm surprised it got through security. I remove the straw from its plastic and jam it in the box. A fountain of purple juice sprays out of the straw with the force of a pressure washer. It gets the top half of my shift dress. I resemble a gross teething baby. My neighbour offers me his single-ply plane-issued napkin, which I use to wipe my chin and pat my chest.

When we finally get to Calgary, I wait at the luggage carousel in denial, hoping perhaps my bag made it to Alberta via large bird. It takes a while for the carousel to start up. People mingle and discuss the flight, its detour, the collective suspicion that a relative of Andre the Giant was sitting in the first row. I don't know why I wait with them. Why I don't identity myself at the baggage claim and explain that my bag was mistaken for the pregnant lady's.

Finally the red light flashes and the carousel lurches forward. Passengers gather around the perimeter watching and waiting for their bags to descend from the chute. One by one they claim their duffle bags and hard shells. The odd cardboard box with St. John's tags.

Eventually I am the last woman standing. A single grey bag makes its rounds unaware that its owner is giving birth somewhere in the GTA. I watch it round the corner and chug closer and closer. My dress sticks to my chest. Sweet grape. It will stain and I won't have any clothes to wear tomorrow and the Mac's at the end of the terminal only sells bananas and Certs. A WestJet employee emerges from baggage claim and walks towards the carousel behind me. It is now just me and the bag. In four seconds it will be in front of me. In six it will have already passed and will be snatched up and sent back to Toronto. I will have nothing to wear to the training in the morning. I haul the bag off the belt and make like a criminal for the nearest exit.

After a short ride to the hotel, I ride the elevator with anticipation to the fourth floor. The suitcase is like a giant grab bag. I rub my eyes leaving makeup smudges on my hands. Once I'm in my room, I haul the suitcase onto the second bed and read the luggage tag: Mallory Pepper.

Inside are stacks of maternity clothes. Pants with big spandex panels. Shirts with empire waists. Seamless stretchy underwear. If I can't get the grape juice out of my dress, I will have to go the training pregnant. I empty the rest of the suitcase and find a hairdryer, a bag of toiletries closed off in a freezer bag, some Mary Jane Crocs, pajamas, which I change into, and a notebook with the Eiffel Tower on the cover.

I retrieve my mini toothpaste and brush from my own carry-on. Wash my face with water only and then my underwear. I soak my dress in the tub with green tea hotel shampoo. Mallory's pajama pants sag, so I tie them off with the drawstring. I turn off the main light, and trip a few times, feeling my way to the bedside table lamp. After I've clicked it on and I'm in bed, I open the notebook and flip furiously through it, but it's blank. I feel twelve. I decide she intended it to be her birthing journal. I turn back to the first page, grab the hotel pen, and write: *7:30pm-ish, EST(?), went into labour over Vermont? Syracuse?* I close the book, toss it in the open suitcase, and begin searching for signs of bedbugs.

It's too late to call the kids. It is almost three back home. I roll over in my bed, manoeuvring my head across the gel pillow, and realize I'm in possession of stolen property. There's still time to call the airline and tell them I mistakenly picked up Mallory Pepper's luggage, but then I will have to take off her pajamas and they are surprisingly comfortable and smell like vanilla. Calming. I think about how late it is and how tired I'm going to be in the morning and fall asleep hoping the rest of her clothes smell like coffee or Red Bull.

I encounter my dress in the bathtub the next morning. It is stiff and still stained. I wring it out and hang it over the curved bar before turning on the shower. I might be able to wear it tomorrow when it has dried. My underwear is still damp from last night so I take the dryer to it and then dress in Mallory's clothes.

I like being pretend pregnant. At breakfast I order bacon and sausage and three eggs and white toast and think about being real pregnant. The heaviness of my belly. The offensive but magnificent feeling of a tiny stranger ramming into my pelvis like an ice breaker. And the sex. So ugly but so good. Glen always on the bottom and me parked on top. Legs of ham and breasts so dense and full I half expected them to start firing Skittles on climax. And the orgasms. Shaky and sweaty and tight. At times I think they frightened Glen, but they undid hours of tension. The hours of disagreeing about how to put together a crib.

After breakfast, my stomach bloats out unencumbered, actually assists in keeping the pants up. By the time I make my way to the hotel's conference room with the digital easel displaying the company logo, I am already walking pregnant. I pick up my name tag and find a seat. A presenter in a navy suit opens his laptop. The first slide of his PowerPoint presentation opens up: Foundations for Operational Excellence. I debate whether to slit my wrists now or wait until the first break.

People file in and take their seats. Some of them wear cowboy boots, others hats. I stare at them and can't decide whether it's a joke. A man vaguely resembling Matt Damon with black plastic glasses sits beside me. I check his feet for cowboy boots. Doesn't have them. His forehead is enormous like a beluga whale. A giant Cro-Magnon white board. I need a marker. He shoots out his hand and introduces himself.

"Carl," he says.

"Claudia," I reply, shaking his hand.

"Prairie or Central?" he asks, removing the liner off an over-sized muffin he's helped himself to from the snack table.

"Maritime actually," I reply.

He looks surprised. "I've been to New Brunswick once," he says, massaging his legs with the heels of his hands. I wonder if this is because his hands are clammy or his quads are sore.

"It's nice out there."

I nod.

"This guy's a pretty good presenter," he says, gesturing towards the man in the navy suit.

We continue to talk until the welcome speech begins. Thanks for coming, directions to the washrooms, instructions for smokers, agenda, what is operational excellence — Carl smells good. I occasionally look over at him. See if he's taking notes or drawing squares or the little barns you draw without lifting your pencil off the page or crossing over any previous lines. At one point I excuse myself to go to the washroom and I forget that I'm supposed to be pregnant and my pants nearly fall down. I yank them up and create a temporary camel toe. This is not going to work, I think. I stall my return to the conference room and pass by the front desk to get a peek at the weather outside. The sun is shining. It looks warm and inviting.

"Is there anything I can help you with, ma'am?"

I turn and face the clerk behind the desk. She looks my size. "Do you have any pants?"

"Excuse me?"

"Do you have any extra pants?"

"Airline lost your luggage?"

I pause before answering. If I say yes I fear I will have her again upon checkout and when she sees me with a suitcase she will think I lied. Unless I tell her my bag was recovered and delivered. If I say no, she will wonder why I'm wearing gigantic pants. I say, "I packed the wrong pants."

She looks at me confused.

"My mom's pants. I packed my mom's pants by mistake. I took them out of the dryer and it was late at night and I didn't check before I put them in my suitcase. She must have added them to my load because I don't recall washing her pants and I got here late last night and didn't have a chance to buy new pants."

I have broken the rules about lying. Good liars keep their replies to a minimum. One word, maybe two.

"So you're going to be a big sister?"

"Huh?"

She looks at the pants with the beige stretchy panel I'm holding together.

"Your mom's expecting?"

"Oh, no my mom's dead."

"Pardon?"

"A deadweight. She's fat. Belly fat. Loads of it. Stressful job. Behind a desk all day, you know? It causes belly fat. And too much processed food. White bagels, instant oatmeal, soup. I keep telling her she needs to change her diet or job or go to the gym, but maternity stores enable her."

"Right," the front desk clerk replies suspiciously. "I'm afraid

I don't have any pants, Ms. —"

"Pepper," I cut in, crossing my arms over my chest to conceal my name tag.

"Thank you, Ms. Pepper, but there is a mall not far from here. I can give you directions."

"That would be great. Maybe I'll get those after this is over." I point towards the conference room.

I slink back into the room and into my seat. Did I ever fuck that up. I am thirty-five and live at home with my fat mom and wear her pants. *Sorry, Mom,* I think. Just in case she can hear my thoughts.

37

By the time the conference lunch starts, I am increasingly uncomfortable in Mallory's big pants. I eat a foot-long sub and three cookies to try and hold them up. Carl joins me for coffee before the afternoon session gets started.

"Is there dinner tonight?" he asks.

"I don't think there's anything planned," I say. "I think we're on our own." I search my bag for my conference agenda but don't find it.

"There's a restaurant just down a bit from the hotel. They have really good Alberta beef. Interested?"

I consider the offer. I am interested. I like beef. Especially when it isn't ground. And the idea of a restaurant that doesn't have a playroom and isn't Boston Pizza is appealing.

"Sure. Dinner would be good." I take a sip of my coffee. It tastes like a Bunn machine.

I head to the side table feeling intoxicated. A cocktail of nitrates, macadamia nuts, and liberty. I imagine Mallory doesn't have kids, other than the one on the way. And that she doesn't have to cut her father's toenails or tell him when to go to bed. That her mother's alive and well and her brother still gives her rides on the back of his scooter. Mallory, I decide, dines with strangers. I haven't dined with a stranger since Glen and I were together or since we've been apart.

I add a flavoured creamer to my coffee.

"When are you due?"

"Excuse me?" I reply, turning to a young man making tea beside me.

"I asked when you were due?"

"Uhh . . ."

"My wife is due a week from today. It's our first," he says. "I'm so excited."

"Congratulations." I look to see if Carl is paying attention. I want to order wine at dinner.

"She has the same shirt," he says, pointing to Mallory's red v-neck. "Do you know what you're having?" He doesn't let me answer. "We're having a girl. Her name is Delilah."

"That's a nice name," I lie.

"What are you having?"

I test my coffee a second time and reply, "We're leaving it a surprise."

The afternoon session drags on. By 4:00 p.m. no one gives a hoo-ha about operational excellence.

"Did I hear you say you were pregnant?" Carl asks, placing his pen and notes in his briefcase.

"No, I'm not pregnant."

"Oh." He accepts this simply, finishes off his bottled water and screws the cap back on. He asks if it's too early for dinner.

"I'd like to go back to my room first and ditch my stuff."

"Okay," he says. "I'll wait in the bar."

I get into my hotel room and flop down on the bed. I check my cellphone. I have a message from Glen asking where Wes's Beaver necktie is, and another from a baggage claim agent at the Calgary airport.

I call the airport first and quickly sort out the details of my suitcase. They will have it delivered to the hotel. Then I call Glen. "Hi, it's me. The necktie is in one of the legs of his jogging pants. It got caught in the dryer. Yes, I left it there,

I thought you'd search a little harder for it than that. Did he get in trouble for not wearing it?" I speak fast. It's the four cups of coffee. "WestJet called. My suitcase is on its way over."

"It didn't arrive with you in Calgary? Did you file a report?"

That would have been the logical thing to do but instead I stole Mallory's suitcase and fled the building.

"I intended to, but I was so tired I just left the airport."

"What are you doing for clothes?"

"I bought some," I reply.

"They give you money for that stuff, Claud. But you have to report it."

"They give you money?"

"Yeah," he says. "If they lose your luggage they have to compensate you until it's located and delivered."

"But they didn't lose it. They must have took it off in Toronto by accident."

"You had a stop in Toronto?"

Technically. "Yes. Anyways, they called, it's on its way to me now."

"Oh. Okay, then."

"How are the kids?"

"They're asleep. They miss you. You should call tomorrow."

"I will."

I hang up.

The airport's close, but I'm pretty sure it's unlikely my suitcase will have been delivered to the hotel in the two minutes since I talked to baggage claim. So I dig through Mallory's suitcase for something suitable to wear for supper and find a print dress. It is navy with white bird silhouettes. I pull it on over my head. On Mallory it probably looked woodsy and nesty. Mama bird. On me it hangs a bit heavy. The birds don't have any big parts to perch on. I wear my own earrings, dangly ones because Joan's not around and can't pull them from my ears. I smooth down my hair and examine myself in the mirror unable to decide whether I look ready for dinner with Carl or pre-natal class with Big Bird.

Carl is waiting for me at the bar as promised. He is attractive despite the big forehead and round-toed black shoes you'd expect someone working at McDonald's to wear.

"Can I get you a drink?" he asks.

"I'll have a Corona."

He orders accordingly and we sit at the bar. We talk casually and watch people in the lobby come and go. Most seem to be here on business. They carry suit bags and laptops and small non-descript suitcases. A team of Lufthansa flight attendants check in. They are all tall and beautiful. Assholes. I think about the predicament of Mallory's suitcase. I have come too far to simply return it. They will ask questions. They will want to know why I am only noticing a full day later that I have the wrong suitcase. They will accuse me of wearing her pajamas.

"Can I get a shot of Sambuca?"

The bartender takes a shot glass from below and fills it.

"Do you want one?" I ask Carl.

His expression indicates he's reluctant to do the shot. He is not twenty-two or wearing someone else's clothes. He's unsure of the meaning of it.

"To operational excellence?" I muster.

He throws his hands up and accepts.

"Another, please."

The bartender lines up a second shot in front of Carl. I

still have my beer in the left hand. We raise our Sambuca and drink. It momentarily calms me. I am ready for beef but Carl is a slow drinker. His beer is still full. I spin on my barstool and knock into him with my legs.

"Sorry," I say. "This stool has a mind of its own."

Carl smiles and makes steadfast eye contact. He barely blinks. In the five or so minutes that follow he does little more than sip his beer and look at me. He has the calm of a well-trained distance runner. Confidence. I feel like I'm running a fucking steeplechase.

I sip quick and fidget. I can't control the volume of my voice and yell, "How's your beer?" Several patrons look to see if this question is addressed to them.

"Good, thanks," Carl says.

I drink a third of mine at once.

Noticing my nerves, Carl asks, "Should we go eat?"

"Yes," I say, disturbed by my own behaviour. It's like I've never been on a date before. I don't even know if I am on a date. This used to be familiar. Before Glen, when I had my own apartment but was still young enough to wear glitter eye shadow and one-shoulder shirts.

The restaurant, like the hotel, is in the neighbourhood of the airport; it's industrial fine dining. Dark wood, club chairs on wheels, wine glasses the size of fish bowls. Paintings of cowboys and steer are framed in gold and lit from above. We order filet mignons. His constant eye contact is giving me heart palpitations.

"So, do you have any children?" he asks.

"Three," I reply. I don't know why I say this but I can't take it back.

"Girls? Boys?"

"Two girls and a boy."

"Nice." He straightens his silverware. "I have a six-year-old. His name is Cooper."

"My son, Wes, is almost five and my daughter Joan just turned three."

"And your other daughter?"

"She's sixteen. Her name is Shammy."

"Shammy?"

"It's a nickname."

The server arrives with a bottle of red that he has me test. My face is so hot I want to splash it in my face.

"Good," I say, nodding. The server tops off my glass and pours one for Carl.

"What's it short for?"

"Shammy? Oh nothing." It's short for asshole.

Another server arrives with our dinner. I eat an asparagus spear without cutting it and gag. I move on to the steak. If I eat, I won't talk. I think of Glen and wonder how he became Sophisticated Bachelor Glen and I became Teen Mom.

"How's the steak?" Carl asks, hopeful.

"The steak is nice." I reply. "It's very tender."

"Best beef in the country. How long have you worked for Loblaws?"

"Since I was seventeen. I started on cash when I was in high school." When Shammy was born? "You?"

"I'm new to the grocery business. Spent ten years at Ford before I was headhunted. I like it though. This industry is a little more predictable." He spreads béchamel sauce across his steak with the back of his fork.

"What do you do in your spare time?"

"I was training for a triathlon but I hurt my knee demonstrating something in one of Cooper's soccer practices." He chuckles. "I'm waiting for an MRI."

I carefully bisect an asparagus spear with my knife. "That's too bad."

"You know what I love though?" He points at me with his fork. "Taking pictures of icicles."

I'm unsure I've heard him correctly. "Say that again?"

"Taking pictures of icicles. Love it."

"Cool."

"You mean cold," he jokes.

I smile.

Carl pulls out his iPhone and begins scrolling across his screen with his clunky thumb. He stops on an image and holds the phone across the table for me to view. Four icicles hanging off a deck board like prehistoric glassy teeth. He looks at his phone, finds another, and holds it out again.

"I took this one in Kananaskis."

This one is a single icicle hanging off a branch. It looks like a railway spike.

"Nice."

"And what about you, Claudia? What do you like to do?" He slides his iPhone back in his pocket.

I don't like it when people use my name. It's too personal. And I don't know what I like to do. Why is this question so hard? Why can't he just ask something answerable like *how old were you when you were ten?* I'm used to answering questions from people under the age of five.

"I like to do stuff." I panic. "Parkour."

"Is parkour street gymnastics?"

"Sort of," I say. "I just started."

The server comes to the table and removes our plates. He asks if we want to see a dessert menu.

"No thanks," we say in unison.

"I'll just finish my wine," I add.

I pick up my glass and let the last of my Merlot trickle down my throat. "What time is tomorrow's session?"

"8:30 a.m."

I feel jet-legged and have the sudden urge to lay my head on the table and take a nap like my father at Christmas. Carl seems to understand this.

"Should we head back?"

"Yes. The time difference is starting to catch up with me." The server returns with the bill.

"I got it," Carl says. "I can expense it."

I shrug. "Okay."

We head back to the hotel and I stop by the front desk to see if my luggage has been returned. Carl waits beside me. He neither says nor does anything suggestive. I find this disappointing. Was it the parkour? I need more time.

"Want to watch a movie?" I ask, but immediately regret it. I really just want to lie in bed and pick my mascara off.

"No, thanks. I think I'm going to go read."

I should be relieved. "What do you mean, you're going to go read?"

"*The Hunger Games.*" He smiles.

I stand there baffled as the clerk brings my suitcase out of the back room. I am losing to a book.

"Katniss and Peeta both win," I say.

Carl's mouth drops open.

"Yeah. And Peeta gets a prosthetic leg."

Carl throws his hands up. I take my suitcase and struggle to open the pull handle. After three attempts I pick it up and proceed to the elevator.

"Fine," he says. "I'll watch a movie."

"I think I might just go to bed." I'm nuts. Or maybe Mallory's nuts, and I've channeled her craziness by stealing her luggage. I've assumed her wardrobe and her neuroses.

The elevator closes with Carl and me both inside. It shakes as it ascends to the fourth floor.

"So now you're just going to bed?" he asks.

"I might watch a movie."

We get out on the fourth floor. I turn left down the hall, drag my suitcase behind me, and stop in front of my room. "Are you coming?"

And he begins to walk towards me, albeit in a total state of confusion.

Inside my room the red message light is flashing. Who is it and why didn't they just call my cell? Carl stands in front of the TV with the remote. I have to call the front desk to figure out how to listen to the message. It's from my dad asking if I know where Mom kept the sewing kit. I can't imagine what he would be sewing or why he would need it. I call him back from the bathroom.

When he picks up, I immediately say, "Dad. Go to bed."

"Claudia?"

I quickly hang up. Carl's checking the movies on the TV. "Comedy? Drama?"

"What's playing?"

"*The Vow, The Help, We Bought a Zoo.*"

"*We Bought a Zoo.*"

He purchases the movie and sits in the chair by the desk. His argyle socks are in shades of blue. The room falls silent as the movie begins and I start to lose my second wind. I forget about competing with *The Hunger Games.* I miss my kids now and feel guilty for not calling them to say good night. But if Glen can be composed and attractive, then so can I. And I already have him in my room. I am thinking like a serial killer.

"This is boring," Carl says.

I agree. "Maybe we should just call it a night?"

"Yes," he says, standing up from his chair.

No! I think.

I swing my legs off the bed to walk him to the door. The
bird dress is heavier than before. I'm beginning to unravel.
"Thanks for dinner," I say. "It was really nice to get out
of the hotel."

"No worries," he replies, slipping on his McDonald's shoes.

"And sorry for blowing *The Hunger Games*."

He forces a smile and goes for the door. Then, out of
nowhere, Mallory returns, or perhaps it's Teen Mom, and I
spank him on the behind. He jumps slightly and spins back
towards me. My eyes widen and blood starts flowing through
my body. I am in control.

Carl grabs my hips and pulls me towards him. His grip is
strong. The way one might hold a jigsaw or a jackhammer.
I cup the back of his head where his hair slightly curls and
pull him towards my face. We kiss and neither of us closes
our eyes. It is raw. Perfect for an airport hotel surrounded by
construction and gas stops with big flags and unlimited pancakes. I push him against the wall between two bolted pictures
of horses. He attempts to pull off my dress but I've tied the
chiffon belt so tight it gets caught going over my face. I finish
pulling it off and toss it down. It falls heavy, all that extra
material designed to support a pair of humans in cahoots for
their last trimester. I go for his pants. His bulging erection
pokes through his pleats like a theatre performer peeking
through the curtains. He takes off his shirt. Our top halves
press together bare. Lips and cheekbones and chests. Coming
together and pulling away. Grazing one moment, smothering
the next until our bodies get hot and he slips off his underwear and I go down on him.

He pulls me up and finishes on my hip then rests his head
against the wall and exhales. Operational excellence. I think
it's over but he rights himself, pushing off the wall with his

upper back, his penis now semi-hard and pointing to the bed like a sloppy directional arrow. He picks me up, half tosses, half places me on the bed. He grunts something about parkour and takes off my underwear. I want it and don't want it. It's too personal but it's also been too long. Carl dives in like he's hunting for Easter eggs. I come quickly. Like I'm pregnant. He sits up and back on his ankles. His penis, now drooping down like an icicle, drips.

A room service cart passes outside the door. Stainless steel dinnerware clinks, shoes shuffle on the short carpet. Carl dresses and kisses me again. A finish kiss. The loot bag. He makes a quiet exit and when he disappears from the room I feel intense and bold and exhausted. Like I just cut a seven-layer rainbow cake with a guillotine. Like I just bought a fucking zoo.

40

The next day I wear my own black cigarette pants, heels, and turtleneck sweater and go back to eating for one. Toast and grapefruit for breakfast. Green tea. Carl's not in the restaurant. I don't see him until I arrive in the conference room and see him setting up his laptop at the front of the room. He smiles as I take a seat near the back. He speaks to the man from yesterday in the navy suit who today is wearing tan. Carl is today's presenter. I feel like the kid on Degrassi who hooked up with the teacher.

Carl opens with an analogy about *The Hunger Games* while I begin focusing my mental energy on what to do with Mallory's suitcase. I contemplate abandoning it in the hotel somewhere but suspect I won't be able to follow through. I wish there was someone to bounce ideas off of. I text Cathy but I forgot to charge my phone overnight and it dies before she can reply. I consider my other options: Dan, Glen, Dad. Dan will judge. Glen will lecture. Dad will look for my mother. I wait anxiously for the first break.

After a hideous group activity and the arrival of a baked goods trolley, Carl calls a break.

I go to my room to call Allison-Jean. When I sit on the bed to pick up the room phone, I notice a pair of glasses on the floor beside the bed, like they were knocked off during a fight. They must be Carl's.

"Is something wrong?" she asks. "Good job Liam! Keep

your fingers relaxed." Piano playing clunks in the background.
"Did you need Dan? Because he's out right now."

"No, actually I needed to talk to you. I need your help."

She pauses. "Sure . . . what's up?"

"I need you to call all of the hospitals with maternity wards
close to the airport in Toronto looking for a Mallory Pepper."

"There are hundreds of hospitals in Toronto."

"Just call the ones close to the airport."

"And what if I find her?"

"Just hang up."

"I couldn't do that."

"Then tell her you're a florist and you're sending her
flowers."

"But then she'll be expecting flowers."

"Then send her some and I'll pay you back."

"Well, who is she? Am I to say the flowers are from you
or from me?"

"Why would you send her flowers? You don't even know
her."

"You just said to send her flowers."

This is turning out to be more difficult than I thought.

She asks, "How do you know her then?"

"I don't really. But I wore her pants yesterday."

"You don't know her? You wore her pants? Why am I sending flowers to a stranger?"

"Sometimes people kiss strangers. And it's perfectly okay."

"You're losing me, Claudia."

"Jet lag. I'll explain it all later. Can you just see if you can
find her and if you do, call me here at the hotel. Room 437,
and leave a message. I'll be back at the meeting. Please?"

"Okay." She sighs. I can hear her pencil as she takes down
my instructions. "What's the hotel?"

"The Sheraton Cavalier. And don't tell Dan."

"And don't tell Dan," she repeats.

"Don't write that part down."

"I didn't."

"Okay. Thanks Allison-Jean. I owe you. Maybe I can lobby my brother into getting you something. What do you need?"

"I'd like a double oven."

"Fine. I'll work on the double oven."

"I'm holding you to it, Claudia."

"Then find me Mallory Pepper," I say.

"Consider it done."

I finish playing Nancy Drew, plug my phone in to charge, and rush back to the conference room. Operational Excellence resumes and I change my focus to what I will do if Mallory is located. If her birth was vaginal then she'll be on the verge of getting discharged. If there were complications, a c-section perhaps, then she should be still in the hospital. I cross my fingers that there were complications. I'm going to hell. Then it occurs to me that if she was flying, she must have gone into labour early and she and her baby would likely be in the NICU. That is the less favourable scenario of the two because sometimes they will discharge the mother and not the infant and I can't exactly call the hospital and ask for Baby Pepper.

A man in a tan suit is presenter of the moment. Carl takes a seat up front. He periodically opens his briefcase and digs around inside. I assume he is looking for his glasses, which obviously fell off his face while we wall-slammed. He goes for the briefcase again. Checks the same side pocket he's searched twice already. I reach into my purse and pull out his glasses. Polish the lenses with my shirt and put them on. I instantly go cross-eyed. I take them off and blink ten times before my pupils recover. Masochism.

After the session finishes for the morning, we are given a
little over an hour for lunch. Carl makes his way to the back
of the room and walks into a chair sending it toppling to the
ground.

"Sorry," Carl mutters to the woman it crashes down beside.
He turns the chair upright. When he reaches my table he is
sweating.

"What's wrong?" I ask.

"I can't see," he says, "did you happen to find my glasses?"

"These ones?"

"Ahh . . . thank God," he says with relief, "these are my
prescription glasses."

"You think? How do you see out of those?"

He puts them on. "You mean how do I see *without* them."
Silence follows. There is too little to discuss.

"I hope last night wasn't too awkward," he says discreetly.

"It wasn't," I reply.

"Maybe we can have dinner again. Tonight?"

"Tonight? I don't know. I have an early flight tomorrow."

"Oh." He looks at me intently. "Can I bring you dinner?"

"Like room service?"

"Yeah. Like room service."

I nod. "Yeah. Sure. Why not?"

"Around six?"

"Six works."

"Okay then." Carl smiles confidently.

I race upstairs. There's no message from Allison-Jean,
but my phone is almost charged. I want to call the kids. It's
almost 12:30 p.m., middle of the afternoon at home and it
feels like weeks since I've talked to them, but the hotel phone
rings and startles me.

I answer on the first ring. It's Allison-Jean.

"Did you find her?"

"Yes, but she has no idea who you are."

"What do you mean? You weren't supposed to talk about me! I told you to hang up or say you were a florist or something."

"I did say I was a florist."

"You spoke to her directly?"

"Yes, and she wanted to know who was sending her flowers."

"Couldn't she have waited until they arrived and read the little card?"

"She's allergic to flowers. She wanted to know what *idiot* was sending her flowers."

"Who's allergic to flowers? It's not like I was going to send her ragweed."

"Well she's allergic to flowers."

"Why didn't you tell her they were a surprise?"

"Like from a secret admirer you mean?"

"Sure."

"Because secret admirers don't send flowers when you have a baby."

"But they could. So who did you say they were from?"

"I said they were from you but she said she didn't know a Claudia."

"Uhhh," I groan. "Allison-Jean, why did you do that?"

"Look, you're the one who made me phone her in the first place. What was I supposed to say? Anyway, the good news is she has no idea who you are. I even tried to remind her that you borrowed her pants."

"No, you didn't say that!"

"Yeah, I did. That's what you told me. Remember?"

"So how did it end?"

"I gave her your cellphone number."

"You didn't."

"I did. Listen, I'm not sure about the wall oven. We talked about expanding the nook and if we do that we're going to replace the windows and Dan wants to get these remote control blinds and I was thinking some nice built-in seating under the windows would be nice so I need you to lobby him for that instead."

"Fine."

"Have a safe flight home. Oh, and Dan said he'd pick you up at the airport. And the exterminator is going to your dad's tomorrow for the bedbugs."

"Good."

I notice the ringer is turned off my cellphone and find I've missed a call with a 416 area code. It has to be her. No one else calls me from Toronto except Capital One. I keep the phone plugged in and call Glen.

"Can't talk," he says right away. "I'm getting ready for a showing."

"What kind of showing?"

"I was offered an opportunity to show a few of my paintings at a gallery tonight."

"But what about the kids? You said you could watch them."

"This is a huge opportunity."

"Yeah, I get that, but who's going to watch them?"

"Relax. Cathy is coming over at six. I'll take them to McDonald's first."

"Well I want to talk to them so call me before you leave."

I hang up irritated. Cathy is mine. It's time to call Mallory Pepper. I dial the number unsure of what to say.

She answers on the third ring. "Hello?"

I slide down the wall until I'm close to the outlet my phone is plugged into. "Mallory?"

"Who's this?"

"It's Claudia."

"Does this have something to do with flowers?"

"No." I wrap the cord of my iPhone charger around my finger.

"Are you with the adoption agency then? Because I already spoke with Brenda and I'm keeping him."

"Him?"

"Arthur."

"You had a boy?"

"Who are you?" she says in an agitated voice.

I pull out the birthing journal from my purse and messily write Arthur's name on a blank page.

"Sorry," I mumble. "I . . . I . . . I accidentally ended up with your suitcase. When you went into labour. On the plane."

"Ahh . . ." she sighs. "Is that why you were trying to send me flowers?"

"Never mind the flowers. I just want to see that you get your luggage back."

She makes a noise that implies she couldn't care less about her luggage. "You can keep it," she says, confirming my suspicion. "The airline thinks they lost it. They have to compensate."

This is not the reaction I was expecting. "But I don't want to keep your suitcase."

"I can't breastfeed," she blurts. "I keep trying and he just won't take it and I'm so frigging tired I peed the bed last night and I washed my face with shampoo and they won't let me leave. Why won't he breastfeed?"

"Hold it like a cheeseburger," I encourage.

"The baby?"

"Your breast. Hold your breast the way you'd hold a Big Mac and shove it in his mouth."

"But I have no milk."

"It will come. It just takes a few days. Just keep trying. It will happen."

"But how should I hold him? I never paid attention to that part in class. I was going to give him up. Now I don't know how to feed him or burp him or swaddle him, or . . ."

"Hold him however is comfortable. And take off his sleeper. Is he wearing a sleeper?"

"Yes."

"Well take it off so he's just in a diaper."

"Just a second," she says. "I'm going to put you on speaker phone."

I hear the baby crying that familiar newborn wail like he's starving, which in this case he probably is.

"Okay, so I took off his sleeper."

"All right, now hold him right up to your breast so you're skin to skin and he's level with your nipple. You don't want him to have to strain to reach it."

"Like this?" she asks.

"Yes, like that," I respond, hopeful. "Now hold your breast like a cheeseburger and rub your nipple gently across his mouth. When he opens, shove it inside."

I hear her breath. Arthur whimpers. The afternoon session of Operational Excellence is scheduled to resume in five minutes. The baby is silent.

"Is he sucking?" I ask.

"I think so."

"He's on your breast?"

"Yeah, he's on."

"Okay, if he's on properly it shouldn't hurt."

"It doesn't hurt."

"Now look below the jawline underneath the ear. Watch it. If he's swallowing you'll be able to tell."

"He fell off."

"Okay, don't panic; just go back to the cheeseburger."

"Go back to the cheeseburger," Mallory repeats. Then she hollers with jubilation, "He's doing it! He's swallowing!"

Mallory begins to sob. I join her, but quietly. A silent partner.

"No one else has been able to show me how to do it and I was about to give up and now I'm feeding my son," she blubbers. "I'm so tired." She continues to cry. "And I'm constipated and I haven't washed my hair in three days and they keep serving me broth and two percent milk for breakfast and lunch and all I want is an Egg McMuffin and some roast beef or something and they won't let me go home because he's lost too much weight and I look fatter now than before I gave birth."

"Mallory, just feed your baby. When he's finished put his sleeper back on, wrap him back up in his blanket, and put him in his bed. He should sleep well after a good feeding and then go to sleep. Take all the medication you can and then sleep for as long you can. Understand?"

"Okay," she says, blowing her nose.

"Can I ask you a question?"

"Uh-huh."

"Did Arthur arrive early?"

"Thirty-seven weeks. I fibbed a bit at check-in. I just wanted to make it home. I didn't want to give birth alone."

I nod, understanding. "About your suitcase then. What should I do with it?"

"Keep it," she insists. "There is really nothing of value in there. I mean, maternity clothes — what am I going to do with those now?"

"But what about your hair dryer and makeup and stuff?"

"Like I said, I already put in a claim. They're going to give me money for all of that."

"Okay." I stare at Mallory's open suitcase. The mass of maternity wear. The hair dryer I will keep since I buried mine in the yard. "Now that he's latching your milk will come in and when your milk comes in he will start gaining weight and you'll be able to go home."

She takes a deep breath and exhales into the phone. "Are you pregnant?"

The question catches me off guard. "No," I reply. "Not at all. Why would you think that?"

"Your sister said you wore my pants."

"I . . ."

"It doesn't matter," she interjects. "You taught me how to feed my son. Thank you, thank you, thank you."

"You're welcome," I reply, overwhelmed. "And thank you too."

"For the pants?"

"The pants, yes.

"Goodbye, Mallory."

"Goodbye, Claudia."

I press the off button and hold the phone to my heart. I'm a tiny pink tulip of hope.

I head back down to the conference room and attend the remainder of Operational Excellence. I make a cup of Red Rose tea with a handful of creamers. Like Mallory, the hotel has no milk. I wonder about Arthur. His birth weight. His middle name. Does he have a grandma?

When the conference finishes, I go back to my room and kneel between my suitcase and Mallory's, deciding what to keep. I leave behind her personal items, like her makeup and underwear. I fold the pants into a neat stack and place them on the floor. They too will stay in Calgary. I repack the hair dryer, some of the socks, a shirt, and her birthing journal, which I intend to complete with what little information I've gained.

It's just after six and I'm hungry. I wait anxiously for Carl. At ten after he knocks on the door. I feel giddy.

"Hope you like Vietnamese," he says, supporting a well-packed plastic bag.

"Love it," I reply.

He walks past me and sets the bag on the table. "Sorry I'm a few minutes late. I had to go back and get knives and forks."

"No worries."

Carl serves up a spread of vermicelli, pho, shredded chicken, pork. It smells of lemongrass and chillis. It is excellent. He pours mineral water into two paper cups. I twist noodles around my fork. Carl's eyes are magnified behind his glasses. My phone rings.

"That's probably my kids," I say, answering the phone with an enthusiastic mom voice. The kind of hello that if edible would be dipped in chocolate and dusted with powdered sugar.

"Holy fuck, Claudia. You've got to get the hell home."

"Dan?" His voice is loud enough for Carl to hear. I turn my back so the volume might be minimized and then move to the bathroom. "What are you talking about? I'm coming home tomorrow. You're picking me up."

"I'm at Dad's."

"Why are you at Dad's? Is something wrong? Is he dying?"

"Worse than that."

"What do you mean *worse than that?* Worse than dying?"

"Claudia, I talked to the exterminator and he's refusing to do anything. So I came over here tonight to see for myself."

"Why? Where's Dad? Allison-Jean said the exterminator was coming tomorrow."

"Dad's curling. The exterminator had a cancellation today!"

"What is going on, Dan?"

"There is stuff everywhere."

"What kind of stuff?"

"I have to go."

I hang up stunned and uncertain. Uncertain why the exterminator won't do his job and why it's my problem and whether Dan will still be picking me up from the airport tomorrow.

I return to the table not a tulip. Carl has eaten the pho. The vermicelli and the magic are gone. Dan swallowed it. I stare at my pair of suitcases wanting to go home but not back to my life. Carl pushes the last spring roll in my direction. There is a noodle on his eyebrow. How did it get there? I take the spring roll, dip it in the accompanying sauce, and realize this is the last of Carl. For me, that is. The last of Carl and me, or, rather, there will be no Carl and me. He wipes his enormous food-slicked face vigorously with a napkin, and I've had a one-night stand with a manatee.

I arrive back in Halifax after a long flight, feeling weary and disoriented. I make my way off the plane unable to remember anything about Operational Excellence other than dripping icicles. My brother paces at the gate.

"What took you so long?" he accuses. "The board said you landed twenty minutes ago."

Around me people embrace.

"Nice to see you too," I reply.

"Let's go," he demands, turning in the direction of the parking lot.

"I don't have my bags!" I holler after him.

"You took a suitcase?" he argues. "You were only gone for two days."

I ignore him and find the right carousel. Dan opens his mouth to say something, but I tell him not to talk to me. He acts disgusted when I pull two bags off the belt and load them onto a luggage cart. We walk to the car in silence. He opens the trunk.

"I'll do it," he says, wrangling one of my bags.

I drop my suitcase and wait in the front seat. We exit the airport and drive down the highway. We continue not to talk until we reach the suburbs.

"Where are we going?" I ask.

"Dad's."

"I'm not going to Dad's. I want to go home!"

"It will only take a minute."

"I just want to see my kids."

He drives with intent, eyes fixed on the road in front of him until we pull into the driveway of our parents' home.

"He's not even home," I comment, noting Dad's car is not in the driveway.

Dan puts the car in park and motions for me to follow him up the front steps. I do so with trepidation. There's a Canada Post slip on the door. He ignores it. "Plug your nose," he warns.

I am confused. "What for?" I start to panic.

Dan unlocks the door.

"Holy fuck!" I say, grabbing my nose.

Dan looks at me, crazed. His voice cracks when he says, "See?"

I survey the front hall and what I can see of the living room. "What the fuck!"

"I know!" Dan says.

I gag loudly. Stand in shock at the entrance to the house. "Oh my God."

Dan turns around, towards the street. "There's Dad!" He points to our parents' green Taurus, but Dad stops before coming up the driveway. We make eye contact. But before either Dan or I can react he speeds away, tires squealing.

"Close the door," I say, crying.

Dan obliges and covers his face. We stand on the front step. "That is why the exterminator refused to do anything."

I cover my mouth with disbelief. "We'll have to call those junk people."

"Junk people? We need an arsonist."

"Did you go into the bedroom?"

"No, I didn't make it past the living room."

I text Glen and tell him I'm delayed. I look at Dan. "We should see what we're dealing with."

"Isn't it obvious?"

"Yes, Dan, it's a little bit fucking obvious, but maybe, just maybe, it's contained to the front of the house."

I gather my shirt up around my nose. "You go first," I order.

"I'm not going first."

"Geez, Dan, just open the friggin' door."

Dan turns the knob and I push by him and step inside. It's like walking into a dumpster with curtains. Trails, hip-width and head-high, tunnel from the front entry, their walls constructed of boxes, flyers, and unmarked bags. They are graffitied with pieces of my mom's good china, plastic cutlery, clothing, unopened packages of paper towel, mouse droppings. An inflatable swan pool toy is on top of the piano. And it smells like a garbage strike. Of rotting papaya, chicken wings, and hair products. A warren for Vaudeville spirits, heroin addicts, my father. It is devastating.

Something moves. A mouse or a cat. A Gruffalo. I can't see it, nor can Dan, but we know we are not alone.

"How did this happen?" I ask. "Don't you visit him?"

"Don't you visit him?" Dan spits back.

"I see him, but he always comes over."

"Why do you think that is? Maybe because our father decided he would collect garbage."

"It's not all garbage," I attempt to rationalize. "See over here? Brand new Doggy Steps. Still in the package. Check this out." I read the side of the box, "Doggy Steps is essential for pets with hip dysplasia, arthritis, or simply old age, giving your pet freedom from the floor — and more COMPANIONSHIP than ever before!"

"He doesn't have a dog."

"Are you sure about that? I mean there easily could be one hiding in here."

"He does not have a dog."

"Maybe he bought it for the mice."

"Claudia!"

We kick our way through the living room into the kitchen. It is also sick. Festering with rotting food, dishes food-stained in shades of grey, empty cans of Coke Zero, beans, and tuna, an unopened package of Bumpits.

"We have to get rid of everything," Dan proclaims. "Call one of those junk places and get them to clear it out." He swings his arms wildly. "Like what the fuck is that?" He points to a basket of fur on the kitchen table.

"Beats me. Looks like they were strawberries at one point."

"Why would he do this?" Dan drops his head.

"He probably has dementia."

"Dementia is forgetting whether he sent out a birthday card or not knowing how to get to the garage. It is not leaving lasagna under the piano and buying a giant emery board for a cat that doesn't exist."

I look around for the giant emery board.

"I'm leaving," he says. "I will call the junk people. You can meet them here when they come."

"Whoa, why do I have to meet them here?"

"Bedbugs you said were my gig. Garbage is yours."

"Yeah, but there are bugs here too," I argue.

Dan furls his eyebrows. "I'll call you when they're coming."

"Well, what about now? What about Dad?"

"What about him?" Dan hollers. "He can stay here. Apparently he likes it this way."

"He's obviously sick."

"He's disgusting."

"Yes, Dan. It is disgusting, but he's sick. Hoarders are sick."

"Hoarders should be shot."

"How can you say that?"

"Look at this place! This was our home. How could he do this to us? To Mom?"

"This isn't about us! It's about him. He's obviously fucked up."

"Then you stay and sort it out with him. You get him some help."

Dan storms out, slipping on a stack of flyers. He kicks at them and barrels out the door. I follow and watch from the front window. He goes to pull out of the driveway then slams on the brakes. The trunk pops open and he heaves my bags out and dumps them by the edge of the lawn. He slams the trunk back down, but before returning to the driver's seat, he runs up on the lawn, picks up one end of the broken swing, and launches it in the air. It swings back at him and hits him hard in the hip. He says something I can't make out and starts wildly kicking the seat before finally getting back in his car and speeding away.

I look back at the living room. Try to recall moments created here. Those spent lip-syncing to INXS or spying on Dan when he had friends over. Opening Christmas presents. They are buried now. Contaminated.

I go back outside into the fresh air, sit in the dark on the step, and wait for Dad to return, but he does not.

Glen calls. "Where are you?"

"I'm at my dad's."

"You said you'd be quick. I have to work in the morning."

"I'm coming."

I arrive home in a cab. The driver carries my bags to the door. He is polite and I give him a large tip. Inside Glen has his jacket on.

"Your flight landed almost three hours ago. What took you so long?"

"I told you I had to stop at my dad's."

I notice the Welcome Ho sign my kids made for Grandma on the table, but now it's Welcome Home: the "m" and the "e" have been added in blue sparkle gel.

Glen pulls his keys from his pocket. "Well thanks a lot. I agreed to bring them here to save you the trip, but I have work to do. The least you could have done was come straight home."

"Just go," I say. "Get out of here."

"That's it? No 'Thanks Glen for watching the kids'?"

"You want me to thank you for watching your own kids? Sorry that was such an inconvenience. Just leave." I want to hit him.

He walks out and I lock the door behind him. I stumble over my luggage, overwhelmed and tired, and check on the kids from their doorways. I don't risk waking them. I remove my bra in the hall, unzip Mallory's suitcase, and pull on her pajamas.

I wake up the next morning with Joan curled up at the end of my bed. Like a cat squirrel. I slide her up beside me and pull the blanket over her legs, which are cold to the touch. I go to the bathroom, and then check on Wes. He opens his eyes when I enter his room.

"Mommy?" he mumbles, confused.

"It's me," I assure him. "I'm back."

He smiles through a yawn.

I give him a hug. "Miss me?"

"Of course. Can we have pancakes?"

"I have to check if we have syrup. I heard Cathy got to babysit you last night."

"Uh-huh. And we made cupcakes."

"YOU got to make cupcakes? I don't believe you."

"I'll show you!" He throws back the covers, runs to the kitchen, and points inside the fridge. "See? We brought some home for you!"

A tray of pint-sized cupcakes takes over the middle shelf. They are covered with lumps of white icing and black sugar.

"Those look spectacular!"

Wes jumps. Joan appears in the hallway, rubbing her eyes. I tell her good morning and she comes into the kitchen. She smiles at the open fridge.

"Cupcakes!" she says.

I pick her up and give her a good squeeze. "But not for breakfast."

I turn on Treehouse and make pancakes from a box.

"Do we have school today?" Wes asks.

"Yes, but we're going in a bit late."

Dan calls. "The junk people are coming this morning."

"What do you mean this morning? I *just* got home. It's 8:30 a.m. How did you even call them already?"

"I left a message last night and said it was urgent."

"When are they coming?"

"At 10."

"Is Dad going to be there?"

"Don't know, don't . . ."

"Care. I know you don't. He didn't even come home last night."

"He must have because his car was there this morning."

I hang up.

"Was that Grandpa?" Wes asks.

"No, it wasn't Grandpa."

We finish breakfast and I dress the kids for daycare. I throw on paint clothes. Wes asks, "Are you a painter?"

"No, honey. I am not a painter."

"Then why are you wearing those paint clothes to work?"

"I'm actually going to Grandpa's to help do some cleaning."

"How come?"

"Because he needs some help."

"Can I help?"

"Sorry, bud. It's a grown-up job."

"I want to be a grown-up."

"No you don't. Not yet, anyway."

"How come?"

"Because sometimes being a grown-up sucks."

"But why?"

"It can just suck, Wes. Like you have to go to work and look after people and sometimes you have no one to play with."

He sighs dramatically.

"Can me come?"

"No, Joan. You can't come either."

"Because of the bugs?"

"No." Yes. "Come on. Put your shoes on. Let's get to school."

I drop them off and get back in the car. It occurs to me I might get trench foot wearing my sneakers in Dad's house, so I go to Zellers and buy a pair of rubber boots. I also find packages of 3M face masks and medical gloves in the pharmacy. The cashier observes my purchases curiously. I get to my father's house fifteen minutes before the junk people are scheduled to arrive. Dad is not home. I text Dan and ask where he is.

Allison-Jean picked him up, he replies. *I'm on my way.*

I thought you weren't coming? I write back.

He doesn't respond but arrives several minutes later wearing head-to-toe nylon and rubber gloves.

"Are you wearing a snowsuit?" I ask.

"It's a tracksuit."

"Why, are you planning on going for a run in the kitchen?"

"I didn't want to ruin my good pants."

"Are your good pants the ones with the pleats?"

"Claudia, grow up. It's going to be a long day, so can you just close your mouth?"

I open a package of gloves as a large blue truck with JUNK written across its side in white block letters pulls up. A bear-sized man gets out of the driver's seat. He looks like I expected. Tall, wide, gnarly hair. He extends his hand to Dan first and then to me.

"Should we get started?" he asks.

Dan quietly asks whether he's been briefed about the circumstances. He smiles affirmatively.

"It happens all the time with old people."

Sure, when the old people have no kids and live in a shed in rural Montana.

"He's only sixty-three," I say. Dan glares at me. The junk man, Lenny, returns to his truck to retrieve his partner and a pair of industrial-looking work gloves.

"Why did you say that?" he whispers. "We could have at least pretended he was ninety."

"It's just weird thinking of Dad as old. He's only sixty-three. If he's this bad now, can you imagine what he's going to be like when he's ninety? You and Allison-Jean will have to build a wheelchair ramp and one of those easy-access bath tubs."

"Me and Allison-Jean? No, no, no. That is . . . no, absolutely not. Nope." He shakes his head.

"Well I could never do it. I could never afford it, and besides there is only one of me and there are two of you."

Lenny checks the door and finds it still locked. Dan, red-faced, pushes past me with his key. He is so angry he forgets to pull his mask up and gags loudly when he enters the front hall. I put on my mask and rubber boots. Dan yells for me.

"Why would you do that outside for the neighbors to see?"

"Like they don't see the giant truck with JUNK printed on it?"

"For all they know it could be regular household stuff we're getting rid of. Building materials, a broken toaster. You make it look like we're recovering bodies."

"We probably are!"

He makes his angry teeth and summons me in, gagging

again before having the sense to slide his face mask over his nose.

"Whoa!" Lenny says, surveying the living room and what he can see of the kitchen. "This is probably going to take a few days."

"A *few* days?"

"We could try for less," Lenny says, carefully making his way through the house. "If we work around the clock we could be finished tomorrow morning, but that depends on how quickly we are able to get rid of stuff."

"That should be easy," Dan butts in. "Most of it's going."

"Well not *most* of it," I argue. "We're keeping a lot of it."

"Like what?" Dan asks, pulling his rubber glove securely over the sleeve of his track jacket.

I look around. "Like that curtain rod up there."

"Fine, we'll keep the curtain rod."

"And the Doggy Steps!"

"What the hell for? He doesn't have a dog."

"You could use them for Emma. She could use them to get into her crib."

"She can't walk."

"Then I'll take them."

"You don't have a dog."

Lenny starts loading obvious garbage into an oversized bag. Flyers, a soiled pillow, remnants of a Sobeys roast chicken dinner.

"I might get a dog."

"So you'd get a dog but you wouldn't take in your father?"

I grab the Doggy Steps and check the outside packaging for evidence of anything nasty, then carry them outside and place them beside my car. Back inside, Lenny and his partner work aggressively. Trashing and sorting and asking for direction.

"What's this?" Dan asks, holding up a box with a poodle and a walkie-talkie on the front.

"I don't know. It looks a like a baby monitor or something. Flip it over."

Dan does. "The Bark Buster," he reads.

"The Bark Buster?"

"That's what it says."

"What does it do?"

He reads under his breath for a minute then says aloud, "It stops dogs from barking. There's no way he has a dog . . . is there?"

I pause to consider this.

"There are feces in the kitchen," Lenny offers.

He says it in such a nonchalant way that both Dan and I stop and stare at each other.

"Did he just say there were feces in the kitchen?"

"I think so," I nod.

"I can't do this," Dan says shaking his head wildly. "I . . . I . . . I . . ."

"You have to do this," I interject.

"No. No, I don't. This is not my responsibility. I can clean up coffee cups and empty bottles and whatever the hell that thing is," he says, pointing to a cauldron-like pot hanging from the ceiling by a chain. "But I don't do feces."

He pushes through the front door and disappears. "I don't do feces either!" I call after him.

"He's all yours, Claudia! He's all yours."

Lenny gives me a moment before holding up the next item he wants permission to trash.

"Yep," I nod, without looking. "Get rid of it."

I think about Dan's last comment. I want to believe he means Lenny is all mine. That I can pocket Lenny like a piece

of pyrite, bring him home, and show him off in a bowl on
my dresser. But it's clear he means Dad. Dad is all mine. The
bugs, the big underwear, the old man breath, the bits of food
in his new long hair. My body shakes from the adrenaline.
Lenny takes a sip of his extra large coffee. A pack of cigarettes juts out from his chest pocket. He sees me staring.

"Want one?'

"Yes," I reply, steadying myself from a wave of nausea.

Lenny draws one from the pack and lights it for me. I
flick ash on the floor and realize I'm standing on a picture
of my mother. "Oh, Mom," I say aloud. "You do not want to
see this." I manoeuvre my foot over her eyes like a blindfold.
Lenny works away. All in a day's work.

I leave Dad's at four, exhausted, and take a quick shower at home before leaving again to pick up the kids. Both are drizzly.

"What's wrong with you?" I ask Wes.

He complains of a headache. Rests his head in his hands and scowls from the back seat of the car.

"How about you, Joan, how was your day?"

"Bum-stick."

"Right. Listen, kids. Grandpa is coming to stay with us for a while."

"Like a sleepover?"

"Yeah, like a sleepover. He has to have some work done on his house so he's going to live with us until it's finished."

"He can have my room!" Wes offers, leaning forward in his car seat.

"What's in your mouth, Joan?" I ask, looking in the rear-view mirror. "That's very good of you to offer, Wes, but Grandpa's going to take Joan's room. It's closer to the bathroom."

Wes looks puzzled.

"Old people have to use the bathroom a lot."

"When's he coming?"

"Tonight," I say. A truck pulls in front of me with no warning and I slam on my brakes. "Asshole!"

"You just said asshole," Wes informs me.

"Yes, Wes, I did. And sometimes people are assholes."

"Ms. Patty is an asshole," Wes says.

"Wesley!"

"Well, she is! She told me I budded in line but I was really there first."

"Don't call your teacher an asshole, okay? Joan, *what* are you chewing on?"

Wes tells me, "She found a granola bar by her cubby. It wasn't hers."

I shake my head. "Joan. . ."

"You an asshole."

I drive in stunned silence the rest of the way. Once home, I serve my kids microwave pizza and call Glen.

"I need a hand," I say.

"Can't do it, Claudia. Just sold two paintings and the gallery wants to give me my own show."

"But I'm telling you, I *really* need your help. Dad is coming over and I need help moving the double bed out of the basement and then I need someone to watch the kids while I check back on the junk people."

"The junk people?"

"My dad is a hoarder, Glen."

There is a long pause on the other end of the phone. Then he asks, "What do you mean, a hoarder? You mean he collects things?"

"Like the TV show, Glen. The house is a write-off. He has to stay with me."

He sighs.

"Please, Glen. After this I won't ask you anymore. Just help me get the bed."

"I will help you move the bed, but Claudia, you can't just call whenever you need something and expect that I can do it. I mean I try to help you out when you need help but we're not . . . you know . . ."

"Married? Yes, Glen, we never were. That's not the point. The point is the kids have two parents and right now they need you."

"No, Claudia, that is the point. It's not the kids that need me. It's *you* who needs me, but you can't keep making last-minute demands and just expect me to drop everything at the snap of your fingers."

"Are you going to help me move the bed?"

He sighs again. "I can be there in about twenty minutes."

"And the kids?" He does not reply. "Never mind about the kids. Just help me get the damn bed."

I hang up the phone.

"Okay guys. Daddy's coming over to help me set up Grandpa's bed and then we're going over to Grandpa's house for a minute."

"But I'm tired," Wes complains. "I want to stay home."

"I'll buy you ice cream," I bribe.

"Me too?"

"Yes, Joan. You too."

When Glen arrives, we share few words beyond those associated with moving the bed.

"I can stay and watch the kids for a bit," he offers as I give the mattress a final shove against the wall.

"No, thank you," I say coldly. I close Joan's closet door and throw her stuffies into a round tub.

"Claudia. Don't be difficult."

"Don't be difficult?" My neck tenses and I look into his eyes. Eyes that are becoming less familiar. He wipes his hands on his pants, pants I've never seen before. I'm suddenly aware of the length of our separation. The accumulation of an entire wardrobe. Underwear I didn't buy, pants with pockets I've never emptied before throwing them in the wash. "You don't know what difficult is."

I leave him in Joan's room.

"Come on, kids!" I say in a fake voice.

"Are we going for ice cream now?"

"We are, Wes. Put your coat on."

"Claudia?" Glen says, following us to the door.

"After you," I reply. He obeys, Wes follows him, and then Joan, wearing snow boots. It is twelve degrees outside.

When I pull into my dad's, it is late and approaching bedtime. I tell the kids to wait in the car. They obey and continue licking their soft serve. Lenny and his partner have made progress.

"Hello," he says. "You're just the person I was looking for."

"Sorry it took me a while."

"No problem," he says, pulling off his gloves. "I spoke with your brother on the phone a few times so we're all good. It's just all the stuff against that wall I need help with." He gestures to an obscene pile. I cover my nose. "What of it do you want to keep?"

I examine the pile closer. Cards from Mom's birthday. An old cross-stitch. The afghan we slept under, on the couch, when we were sick. I take an end of the afghan and tug it slightly. It causes an unopened box to tumble from the top.

"None of it," I reply. "I don't want to keep any of it."

"Not even that nice blanket?"

When I make a second attempt to free the afghan, I see that it's covered in oily blotches.

"Not even that," I reply.

"I'll give you a minute. I'm just going to go out to the truck and have my supper." I follow him out to check on the kids. Joan has ice cream in her hair. I do my best to get it out with a napkin.

"Can we go in?" Wes asks.

"Nope. Grandpa isn't home, remember?"

"What does J-U-N-K spell?"

"It spells junk."

Lenny emerges from the truck with his partner. He finishes a banana and tosses the peel in the back.

"I'll be right back, okay, Wes? Joan?"

I follow Lenny into the kitchen. "Do you want the contents of the fridge gone?"

He opens the door so that I can take a good look inside, but I say "Yes" after only a glance.

"Freezer too?"

I open the freezer. There are casseroles stacked on top of each other. I presume they've been there since Mom's funeral. Recipe cards with instructions are illegible under frost-covered bags. The ice smells old. The whole appliance hums.

"Clear it out," I instruct.

Lenny offers me a comforting smile. "Makes it easy," he says.

"Are you okay if I leave?"

"Oh yes," he assures me. "Your brother said he'd be back around nine."

I thank him and navigate my way to the front door. I flip through some unopened mail bundled in the entryway.

"Are you still there?" Lenny calls from the kitchen.

"Yes," I yell back.

"I have something for you!"

"What is it?"

He rounds the corner and hands me a dog. It looks like an Ewok. A mix of pug and Shih Tzu.

"Found him in the bathroom," he says. He pats it lovingly on the head. I stare at Lenny, speechless.

"Good night," he says. "If it helps, he just went to the bathroom."

"That doesn't help," I reply.

As I'm carrying the dog to my car, cradled in my arm, my father's Taurus pulls up to the curb. I notice Joan is asleep as I pass the back seat. My dad is slow to get out of his vehicle. I want to hit him and hug him. Shake him violently, rock him like a baby.

"Dad," I whisper, as he comes up the walk. "Why didn't you say something?"

He reaches out and pets the dog. "I see you found Paul."

"Paul? Dad there is dog shit all through the house! What were you thinking?"

"Not in the bedroom," he argues. "Paul was never allowed in the bedroom."

I stare at him in disbelief. "You should have said something earlier. You should have asked for help."

"I don't want to talk about it right now." He puts his hands up. They tremble.

Wes lets himself out of the car. "A puppy!" he cries.

"Back in the car, Wes."

"But I want to see the puppy!" He makes fists with his hands and jumps.

"BACK in the car," I repeat sternly.

Wes starts to whine.

"I set up a bed for you," I tell my father.

"I'll be fine," he argues, pointing to the house.

"No, you will not be fine. Nothing about this situation is fine. You can't go back in there. You can't sleep there."

"Claudia, I really am fine."

"Just come to my place. At least until it's all cleared out." A next-door neighbour peers through her front window blinds. At the truck. The bits of debris littering the driveway. Seconds later her husband joins her. Dad takes note.

He caves. "Fine. Let me just get a few things."

"I'll wait here," I say.

The temperature drops and wind comes out of nowhere. I shiver. Paul licks my neck. I strain so he doesn't get my lips. My dad emerges several minutes later empty-handed. I get into the car and place the dog on the front passenger seat next to me. Does it have fleas? My father finally gets in his car and sits behind the wheel.

"I didn't know Grandpa got a dog!" Wes exclaims.

"Neither did I, Wes." I don't even know if Grandpa knows he got a dog. I think about Glen with George, Dad with Paul. Am I also supposed to get a pet? Am I allowed to get a dog?

My convoy and I return home close to 9:00 p.m. I carry Joan in first. Accidentally take her to her room before remembering her bed is now in Wes's room. I am sweating by the time I plunk her down. I take off her snow boots and go back out for Wes, passing my dad on the way. I wonder if he will be offended if I ask him to shower.

"So do you have bugs on you? Right now?"

"No," my father replies sternly.

"Can the dog sleep in my room?" Wes asks hopefully. Paul barks as if in agreement.

"No way. Paul is sleeping outside."

As soon as we're in the house, I tell Wes to put on his pajamas, and Paul starts barking.

"Shut up, Paul!"

Dad sits down at the kitchen table. I put Wes to bed, then I join my father.

"Are you hungry? Can I make you anything to eat?"

"No, Allison-Jean made a big roast beef dinner."

"How was Dan?"

"We haven't spoken," he says.

"He's just upset. He'll come around."

I observe my father in search of understanding. His garment of shame is slight; a mere pocket square in a jacket. It pisses me off. I want him to wear it like a Hazmat suit.

"I don't see why this is such a big deal," he says. "My stuff has nothing to do with you or Dan or anyone else."

"YOU HAD SHIT ON THE FLOOR," I say slowly and loudly. "I couldn't step foot in my bedroom because it was filled to the top with NOTHING."

"That hasn't been your bedroom for nearly twenty years!"

"You had to have an exterminator!"

"I didn't need one!"

"You got bedbugs!

"They weren't bedbugs!" he says, slamming his fist on the table. The movement sets one of Joan's mechanical hamsters into motion. Like a lemming, it wheels itself right off the table. Paul runs in the room and sniffs it on the floor. "Dr. Harvey said it was just a skin infection."

"Yeah, well no wonder you got a skin infection. The junk people are coming back tomorrow. I think you should be there." I get up from the table. "I think you should go to bed now."

I get up early the next morning and drive to Walmart to buy my dad a few things. Large underwear, deodorant, a package of Stanfield's undershirts and track pants because I don't know his exact size. When I return home, I place the items on the table and make him breakfast. I suggest he give Paul a bath. Joan is enthralled with the dog.

"Keep?" she asks.

"No, honey. Paul is Grandpa's dog." I pick Paul up. "He doesn't look like a boy."

"Paul's a girl?" Wes asks. "Can we change his name?"

"Grandma," Joan suggests.

"No, we are not naming the dog Grandma," I tell her.

"What was Grandma's name?" Wes asks. He traces the liver spots on my dad's hands.

"Janice," Dad answers.

"What about her middle name?"

"Mildred." Dad chuckles. "After her own mother. She hated that name."

I flash back to the photo of Mildred that Dan gave Mom for her birthday.

"I don't mind it," I say. "Anyway, the dog already responds to Paul. It's short for Pauline. We're not changing its name."

Joan takes her oatmeal to the floor and eats beside the dog. "Hi, Janice," she says.

"Paul, Joan. Her name is Paul."

She fishes out a handful of oatmeal and attempts to feed Paul. "Here, Janice," she says.

"Joan!" I look for my father to intervene but he's preoccupied picking bacon out of his teeth with the hand of one of Wes's wrestlers.

"Gross," I comment. "Remember, you're supposed to be at home soon. We need to go."

My dad quickly gets his shoes and pulls his keys from his pocket. He gets into his car while I hurry the kids into their car seats. As we're pulling down the driveway, Wes says, "Mommy, I want to have a party for Daddy."

"A party for *Daddy?* Why do you want to do that? His birthday is in August."

"Because he sold some of his paintings and I think we should celebrate."

"That's very thoughtful," I tell him. "But can't you ask for something more reasonable? Like a DS or LEGO?"

"Can I have a DS?"

"No."

He growls. I can't wait to get to work. I spend the morning reviewing a sponsorship request for a theatre group's upcoming production of *One Flew Over the Cuckoo's Nest.* I call the director and say, "Yes."

Cathy and I meet for lunch.

"Wes wants to have a party for Glen."

"What for?" she asks, pushing olives from her salad to the side of her plate.

"Because he sold some paintings."

"Yeah, I saw that in the paper."

"What do you mean?"

"The *Herald* did a story on him."

"When?"

"Yesterday."

"Yesterday?"

"I assumed you would have seen it."

I take one of the olives from her plate. "No, I didn't. I normally read the paper at work but I was off yesterday."

"Travel day?"

"Sort of. I needed to help my father."

"How's he doing?"

I pause before confessing, take a large sip of my Perrier. Then I whisper, "He started hoarding."

"Hoarding?" She looks confused. "Like cats?"

"Why cats?"

"Isn't that what most people hoard?"

"No, like garbage and things. Well, I guess there was a dog living there."

Cathy's eyes widen. She tears open a piece of dark seedy bread and slathers it with butter. "That sounds bad."

I provide her with the lowlights.

She places her knife down. "Geez. That's . . . wow. I'm sorry, Claud. Were there any signs?"

"Not really."

"It's just stuff, though, right? I mean, stuff can be replaced. He's okay?"

"He's staying with me until it's cleaned up."

"Wow," she repeats.

"It's fucked. And on top of all this, Wes wants to have a party. What do I do? I don't want to have a party for Glen. I hate him right now."

Cathy waves down a server. "Could I have some more water, please?"

"He's getting on my nerves."

"That's nothing new."

"And . . ." I lean in. "I think he's frigging seeing someone."

Cathy's jaw does not drop. Her eyebrows do not hit the ceiling. "That was bound to happen at some point. It's been a couple years now, no?"

"Depends on when you start counting. Either way, I'm not ready."

She nods. "When you're ready, I have complete confidence that you will have no problem meeting someone."

"I mean I'm not ready for *Glen* to move on." I consider telling her about Carl as proof of my own readiness to move forward, but the memory is uncomfortable. Is this why she is still single? Is it simply a matter of "readiness"?

"Just throw the party, Claudia, keep it simple. Don't over-think it. Get a cake and some chips and let Wes make him a card."

I sigh.

"Do it for Wes," Cathy says. "And let me get this." She scans the restaurant for our server and sees him at the back entering things on a touch-screen computer. "You hoo," she calls quietly, attempting to get his attention. He does not respond, so she takes her napkin and waves it high above her head. A white flag. Surrender.

I'll have the party.

"So what kind of cake do you want for Daddy's party?"

"Chocolate!" Wes yells from his car seat.

"With sparkles," Joan adds.

"You mean *sprinkles,*" I correct.

"No, sparkles, you idiot!" she says, slapping her legs.

"Joan?" I say with astonishment. "How many times do I have to tell you this? You do not call your mother an idiot!" I stare at her in the rear-view mirror and she half-rolls her eyes. "For that matter you don't call anyone an idiot. Do you even know what an idiot is?"

"A stupid idiot."

"No, an idiot is not a stupid idiot. That doesn't even make sense. It's not a nice thing to call someone an idiot. I don't want to hear you say idiot or stupid."

"Can we say stupididiot like it's one big word?"

"Wes," I say, in warning. "Now I was trying to ask you what kind of cake you want for your father."

"I already told you chocolate." He kicks the back of the seat in front of him.

"WHAT KIND OF ICING?" I ask loudly and sternly.

"Poop icing."

Both kids laugh. I think of my mother when she was the driver and I was in the back seat observing her. Most of the time she had her driving face on: focused and rigid. But the odd time I'd look up and catch her smiling at something I couldn't see and though I never found out what it was, it was always comforting.

"Why are you smiling, Mommy?"

"Just because," I whisper.

Once home, thinking about what to make for dinner, I open the fridge and find the top two shelves stuffed with meat. It looks like a butcher shop. "Dad, do you know why there's all this meat thawing in here?"

"I thought I'd take something out for dinner," he says. He's sitting on the couch, reading.

"Something? There's enough meat in here to feed an army."

My dad suddenly looks nervous. He puts his book down and comes into the kitchen. I've got the fridge open for Dad to see, and Joan systematically starts emptying the door of its condiments, which includes four different kinds of mustard. I look at the kids as if they're to blame for the lot of mustard.

"Who bought all this mustard?" I ask.

"I think it was Daddy," Wes says.

He is of course wrong. Glen hates mustard, but I go with it.

"I think you're right, Wes. And the syrup too. There are two bottles of syrup and both are open. I think Daddy did that too."

"He did," Wes agrees.

What else did Daddy do, I wonder, looking around the house. There is a spot of nail polish on the couch. Glen's fault. The countertops are peeling. Glen. My jacket's abandoned on the floor of the front hall. Still Glen. I could do this all day.

"Seriously, Dad, why did you take all this meat out?"

I go to open the freezer. Dad reaches out like he might intervene. His mouth opens but he doesn't speak.

"What the hell?"

"Sorry," he apologizes nervously. "It's just temporary. Just until I can get back into my house."

"I told Lenny to throw these out!" I remark, counting the stack of casseroles five high and two deep. "Tell me you did NOT take these out of the garbage."

"They were still in the freezer," he insists.

"They are *old*." I close the freezer and survey the farm melting in my fridge. "How are we supposed to eat all of this, Dad? That's a week's worth of meat."

"I'll cook it," he promises.

"Keep your shoes on!" I say as Wesley sits down to yank off his *Cars* sneakers. Joan, hearing the order, kicks her Crocs across the front hall.

"Put those back on."

"You do it," she says.

"No. You kicked them off, you put them back on."

She shakes her head defiantly. I walk over and remove some shitty McDonald's toy from her fingers and toss it in the cupboard above the sink. She shrieks, as I expected she would. I am irritated and hungry.

"Put your shoes back on and you can have it back."

She jumps around and I ignore her. I grab my iPhone and order KFC.

The dinner arrives with a free strawberry cheesecake. I pull it out of the bag and slide it onto the counter. It smells like flavoured massage oil and I hate flavoured massage oil. It's like spraying rose-scented aerosol on a poop. The resulting smell is rose-poop. Cheesecake on a crotch. Cheesecake-crotch. I messily set the table, dumping the napkins and individually wrapped plastic cutlery into a giant heap. I need to get out of the house.

While we're eating, I say to the kids, "Let's do something.

What is something fun that you'd like to do?"

Wes dips a fry in ketchup. "Go to Disney World?"

"Something like that, but a little closer to home."

"Swimming! Let's go swimming."

I check my watch and wonder how late the pool's open.

"Do you think we have time?"

"Yeah, I think so," Wes replies affirmatively.

"Joan, do you want to go swimming?"

She picks out a wedgie and nods her head.

"Okay, here's the deal. If we want to go swimming then everyone needs to cooperate and do what Mommy says. Wes, you go get your swim trunks and put them on — without your underwear underneath — then put your jogging pants and T-shirt back on."

"What about my socks?"

"Skip 'em. Joan, you come with me to get your bathing suit on." I pause. "Dad, wanna come?"

"No, you go," he says. "I'll clean up here." He gestures to the table, partially stands, but it's to take another piece of chicken from the tub.

Joan follows me excitedly to her room. I dig out a Little Swimmer from last summer. She fusses a bit but cooperates as I shove her legs through the small holes. Her thighs bulge outward like the limbs of a balloon animal. I put her pajamas on over top and tell her to wait by the door while I round up towels and get myself ready. I tuck my pubic hair into my suit.

By the time both kids are at the door with their Crocs on, Dad's started cooking the farm for a hundred future meals. I tell him where the Tupperware is. He opens the cupboard releasing a landslide of lids.

"Now, who's ready to go swimming?"

My kids scream "ME!" simultaneously.

I pile them into the car, one car seat at a time, and though the buckle on Joan's seat belt has slipped into the crack at the base of the seat and the subsequent retrieval causes me to flatten my finger like a breast in a mammogram, I remain externally calm. When we get to the pool, the parking lot is empty and I revert to internal motherfucker/asshole commentary. I pull up front.

"Wait right here. Mommy will be back in just a sec."

I leave my door open and head directly for the sign posted on the main door: Close for Mainence. Clearly written by a university professor. I run back to the car and jump inside.

"What's wrong, Mommy?"

"Mommy just went to the wrong pool by mistake. We have to go to the other pool."

"The one with the big pirate ship?" Wes asks, hopeful.

"No, not that one. We'll do that one soon." Soon meaning when he's fifteen.

"What other pool is there?"

"I want to go swimming."

"We are going swimming, Joan. We're just going to another pool instead."

I pull into the parking lot of a Quality Inn with a waterslide visible through the glass roof of the hotel pool.

"Wait right here." I say this again, despite knowing they are trapped between opposing layers of twisted seat belt. They both look at me like *thanks for the suggestion, dumbass.*

I walk into the hotel and go to the front desk, prepared to trade my foot for access to the pool.

"Checking in?"

"Actually no. I'm just wondering, is your pool for public use?"

"It is, as a matter of fact." She gives me the pricing.

"Perfect. I'll be right back."

I haul the kids out of the car and they trudge through the front lobby. Wes drags his Spiderman towel behind.

"Pick that up, hon. It's dragging."

He reels it in with a grunt. I pay the clerk and she gives me a key card and points us in the direction of the pool.

"Wait for Mommy," I say, once we're at the edge of the pool. I try to remove my clothing at the same speed as my children.

Joan asks, "Can me jump in?"

"No."

"Can I go down that?" Wes asks, pointing at the giant red slide. He jumps up and down and his voice wavers with excitement.

"Maybe with me, but let's get in the pool first."

I carry Joan on my hip and descend the stairs. The temperature is comfortable. Nice after a long day. Joan squeezes my neck and Wesley flaps beside me, barely afloat.

"Stay to this side, Wes, where it's shallow."

He flutters back to the shallow end and bravely dunks himself.

"Good job, Wes."

He rubs his eyes furiously then smiles.

After three minutes of frolicking, which feel more like ten, we approach the winding steps up the slide. I read the sign. It appears I have made an error in judgment. Wes is too small to go on his own. Joan should not go period. But I make the decision to see the sign as a suggestion more than anything, and by the time we've ascended the steps, the prospect of taking the stairs in reverse quite frankly frightens me. Panting under Joan's weight, I sit down at the top of the slide, which is essentially a dark tunnel, with Joan between my legs and tell Wes to come in front.

"Now don't move Wes. I'm going to wrap my legs around you so that we all go down together."

But as Wes turns to listen to my instructions his small butt pivots beneath him and he starts down the slide sideways. I grab his arm but instead of stopping his descent the move pulls Joan and me sideways forcing a partial wedgie in my suit. And that is how the ride ensues. I carry the weight of one child and my own body on one dry butt cheek while Wes dangles helplessly from my grasp, absorbing the force of the ride in his knobby spine. Joan is silent for the six seconds of skin chafing, presumably because she is comfortably resting on the fleshy part of my thighs. Wes and I scream. And just when the light from the pool below becomes visible, the ass-hole speeds up and sends us spinning backwards until we are messily unloaded into the water.

I scramble to the surface dragging both kids with me. Wes howls. Joan rubs at her chlorine-stung eyes. She has a long scratch but is otherwise unscathed. I set her on the pool deck, followed by Wes, who accuses me of pushing him down the slide. I turn him around to inspect his back. It is red but not really bleeding. Wes continues to sob softly while I lay out our clothes to get dressed. Shirts first to cover their goose bumps followed immediately by pants as I have managed to forget to bring underwear for any of us.

"Okay," I say, feeling defeated. "That wasn't too much fun, was it?"

Wes shakes his head sadly. It is 8:30 and past their bedtime but I drive fifteen minutes in the hopes Dairy Queen will somehow salvage the night. Two Dilly Bars later the kids are asleep with chocolate on their faces. I put my pajamas on and watch *The Nature of Things* with my dad.

"What are you eating?" I ask him.

"Some of the pork. It's real tasty. Want me to make you up a plate?"

"Why is it shredded like that?" I ask, leaning in for a closer look.

"I pulled it apart with a fork."

"No thanks," I mutter. "Where's Paul?"

"She's outside."

In a moment of pity for Paul, I go out back to check on her. She's wound her leash around a tree. It takes a few minutes to untangle her. When I do, she brings me a pinecone. I squat down and scratch her neck. Brush bits of bark and debris from her back.

"Come on," I say. "Let's go inside."

She treads close behind me.

My dad is asleep sitting up on the couch, a half-empty plate on his lap. The pork has gone hard and slides in a mass towards my hand as I carry the plate to the kitchen.

"Dad," I whisper, returning to the living room. "It's time to go to bed."

Saturday is a big day. My father's house is ready for him to move back in and it's his first major bonspiel. Glen picks up the kids and I go watch. There are more young people in the stands than I expected there would be. A few families with children. Some spectators in their twenties. An odd proportion of people are eating fries. There are four sheets of ice in play. One game is already under way. Three others are about to start. I spot my dad second sheet from the end. His broom is different than those of his teammates. I wonder if this is a good thing or a bad thing. I wish he knew I was watching.

He gets set to play, brushing the bottom of the rock and manoeuvring his foot in the hack. For the moment he is the only action in the rink. He pushes away, releasing the rock. It almost looks graceful. Artful. Until it flies through the house and bumps the back of the sheet. My dad scrambles to his feet with a look of horror. His adopted teammates also assume looks of horror. People around me mumble comments. Two teenagers in front of me laugh out loud.

"Did you see that? What a retard."

"My grandma can curl better than that and she's in a wheelchair."

"My balls could curl better."

They laugh again.

My dad gets a comforting pat on the back from one of his teammates. He wipes his hands on his pants and returns to

the hack for his second shot, preceded by action on the neigh-
bouring sheet. When he gets set to release, all eyes are on him.

The teenagers nudge each other and look in my father's
direction. This time his rock doesn't make it to the hog line.
No rocks for Gerald.

"What a loser!"

"I told you, he's a retard."

I start to panic for my dad. I want to tell him it's okay the
way he did when I fell off my bike or failed a spelling test.
It's only the first end. Refocus. Kill yourself. But I can't get
to him. I can, however, get to the teenagers in front me. I can
wipe my boots on their hoodies for instance.

"That guy is a total pussy."

"Loser."

"Excuse me," I say. The blond one on the left looks up. He
has an excessive amount of product in his hair. "Don't you
think it's a little *uncool* to be watching curling?" I ask him.

He stares up at me bewildered. Unsure what to make of
the question. I panic, suddenly worrying his parents may be
close by.

"What?" he replies, after exchanging looks with his friend.

"Like, don't you think it's a bit loser-ish to be hanging out
watching a bunch of old guys throw rocks?" I make an 'L' with
my right hand, subtly bring it to my forehead, and whisper,
"L . . . o . . . s . . . e . . . r."

"Fuck you." He takes a swig of his fountain pop and motions for his friend to leave with him.

"I'm just saying." I lean back in my chair. Watch momentarily as my dad successfully sweeps a rock into the house.

"My dad's the provincial champion."

"My dad's Kevin Martin," I reply.

The teenagers stand up. Noticing their row exit is blocked

by some seemingly purposeless caution tape, the pair is forced to climb over their seats. I contemplate sticking my foot out to trip them. Preferably the blond, but I have already stooped to an unconscionable level. They at least were acting their age. He turns around and says, "Cunt!"

No one has ever called me a cunt before. It makes me feel old and dated. Why couldn't he have called me a pussy?

The arena erupts into cheers and whistles. I clap along observing the time on the giant digital clock. It could be hours before the game's over. I decide to leave the stands and head to the bar for a drink, hoping to find the happy masses.

I am not disappointed. The rink lounge is exactly as I imagined. The happily unfit drink Moosehead on dated leather-tacked pub chairs, cajoling each other. I order a pint. Sit at the bar and browse through a curling supply catalogue. Glance at the side wall, which is lined with tarnished trophies, photos of foursomes, banners behind glass cases. I could kill hours here. Drinking draught and listening to stories. Periodically I give my two cents. It's that kind of place. I keep meaning to return to the game to check on my father's progress, but I feel heady and drunk and everyone's happy.

A man enters the lounge and orders an orange juice. His peers address him as Tony.

"What's going on out there, Tony?" they ask.

"Games are all over," Tony replies.

"Already?"

A few of them check their watches

"Geez, it's that late already."

One of them asks if Don is still around.

"I think he's on his way up," Tony informs everyone. He gets closer to one table in particular and bends in. "There's a guy still out on the ice, won't come off."

"What? He's protesting a call or something?"

"No." Tony's eyes widen. "He's just lying on the ice."

"What a loser!" I offer, slipping partially off my stool.

A few of the men look at me.

Someone asks, "Are you sure he's not having a heart attack or something?"

"No, no, he just won't get up off the ice."

"Oh, you mean he's actually lying on the ice." The guy who asks this has a large moustache. He demonstrates the scenario by laying his hands on the table.

"Lying on the ice," Tony repeats.

"Maybe he needed a nap!" I offer, laughing at my own wit.

I realize with a little alarm that the tail of my shirt has caught on my stool.

Tony takes a sip of his juice, lowers his voice. "Someone said he was crying."

In a second I am sober and heading down to the ice.

My dad has no expression. If there were tears at one point, they've since dried up. I crouch down beside him. "Hey, Dad," I whisper.

"Claudia?" He lifts his head exposing an ice-pink cheek. Like a blot of colour in a black-and-white film. It is the only youthful thing about him. Everything else declares age. His jellyfish-pale skin, the grey-blue of his veins.

"Claudia," he says again. "You came to watch?"

"I did."

The arena is still. Quiet but for the hum of the overhead lights.

"I *just can't* seem to do it without her. I tried and I just can't."

I brush snow from his knee.

"I tried to cook a ham and I put it in the oven with the

plastic wrap still on it and I don't remember what vitamins to take and when because there's an order. There are night vitamins and there are morning vitamins and you can't mix them up because some of them don't go together and then they don't work the same so you have to get it right and I *just can't* get it right." He talks with his hands in the air.

"You don't have to do everything the way Mom did. Just because it was her way doesn't mean it was the right way or the only way, it was just that — it was *her* way. Except for the ham. You don't cook it in the bag."

I want to lie down. I have the spins. But my dad is making progress, and I don't want him to retreat, he's pushed himself up onto his elbow. He sticks out his hand. I help him to a seated position. He reaches forward, pulls his sock down a little, and scratches around his ankle.

"Your socks are way too tight!" I say, running my finger over the trench left behind from the sock's elastic. "Why would you wear those?"

"They're brand new."

"Are you sure they're for men?"

He examines his socks. Runs his finger around the perimeter of the opening.

"Well, they were right next to the men's underwear."

"Huh," I say, surprised. "You should take them back."

My dad manoeuvres himself onto all fours and gradually rises to his feet, eventually pulling me up with him. We stand in the button. A one-foot white circle that feels remarkably like an epicentre. I cling to him, drunk and dizzy.

"Where's your stuff?"

He motions to a duffel bag, rinkside.

"I need you to drive home."

"I can see that," he says, giving me the once-over.

A maintenance person looks relieved to see my father on his feet, but once we're headed his way he puts his head down and busies himself behind a score table. We exit the building in silence.

It's a dreary scene outside. Beige cars and cracked asphalt. Shapeless clouds strewn across the sky. Dad opens the passenger door of his Taurus and helps me inside, as though I've just given birth or something. For the moment he has purpose. Some responsibility. A job. One that he knows. I crank my seat back to a reclined position as he pulls into reverse. I look over and catch him smiling. And in that moment everything feels light and lifted. Hair blowing in the wind. A song by ABBA. Expression has returned to my father's face and I savour it. Like replacing an overturned rock back on the dented earth from which it came. Concealing once again its secrets. Potato bugs and centipedes. Debris. I close my eyes.

We don't talk about curling at breakfast the next morning. My dad wears his hair in a ponytail and eats bread with Chia seeds.

"Can you watch the kids?" I ask my father.

He nods and sips his coffee. "Where are you going?"

"To the paint store."

"Don't forget about your car," he says.

I did forget about my car. It's at the rink. I text Cathy and ask her to pick me up. She arrives within minutes.

"Invite her in," my dad says.

"No," I say. "She has a golf lesson. Besides, she's coming tonight."

"We're having company?"

"Glen's party."

"Right," he says enthusiastically.

"I won't be long. Wes, Joan, Mommy's going out!"

Wes calls from his bedroom, "Pick a number between twenty-one and forty-four."

"Twenty-seven."

"Slap yourself in the face twenty-seven times."

What the fuck? I take a piece of Chia bread and run out to Cathy's car. She is wearing a visor and a white golf shirt.

"You called me just in time," she says.

"Yeah, thanks," I reply. "I totally forgot about my car. What time's your lesson?"

"Ten. I was ready sooner than I expected."

"Since when did you take up golf?"

"One of my clients convinced me. Said with my height and strength I'd probably have a long drive."

"I can see that."

"But it's hard. It hurts my back having to hunch over. Especially putting."

"Maybe your clubs are too short."

"That's what my mom said."

When we get to the curling club there are no cars in the back parking lot other than mine. Cathy pulls up beside it.

"Are you still doing parkour?"

"No, it finished last week. It was fun though. Want to see something I learned?"

"Sure," I say.

Cathy backs up and re-parks the car away from mine. She undoes her seat belt. "K, watch this."

She walks about twenty feet away, stops, turns to face the car and then starts running. She makes fists with her hands and they swing high by her forehead. She gets closer and closer and for a second I crouch as though she is going to dive through her open window and tackle me, but instead she hurdles and cartwheels over the hood. When her feet hit the ground she says "whoo!" and adjusts her golf shirt, which had bunched upwards on her sports bra.

I get out of the car and clap. "*Very* impressive."

She catches her breath and gives me the kind of light hug exchanged between competitors at the end of a race.

"Thanks for the ride," I say. "Let me know how your golf lesson goes."

She says, "Will do," gets back in her car, and honks her horn twice as she pulls away.

I skip Home Depot in favour of a specialty paint store I've

passed from time to time and have always wondered about. Here I hope the person will be forced to smile and act patient through my indecisiveness. I arrive just as the store opens. The guy behind the counter looks up from some paperwork and smiles. His T-shirt is faded blue and his hair sticks up and to the side. Kind of preppy, except he has holes the size of quarters in both earlobes. The earrings look as though they might pop out like wine corks.

"Do you need some help?" he offers.

"I want to paint my kitchen."

He comes around from the desk and wipes his hands on his cargo shorts, which are covered in paint. "Tell me about your kitchen."

No one has ever asked this before. It seems personal. Like I'm about to get a breast enhancement and we've come to the part of the appointment when the doctor carefully opens the gown and examines the breasts and then draws on them with a felt pen.

"It has a fridge," I say.

"Black, white, stainless steel?"

"Yellow."

"Yellow? Seriously? Other appliances too?"

"No. Dishwasher and oven are both white. Toaster is stainless steel, microwave is black."

"Do you have one of those built-in can openers too?"

"Negative."

"Continue," he says, playing with his goatee. His eyes are cinnamon brown.

"It used to have a border."

"Floral?"

"Roosters."

"Cabinets?"

"Oak."

"Floor?"

"Beige."

"Backsplash?"

"White tile."

"All white or are there some decorative cornucopias thrown in the mix?"

"Some decorative cornucopias." I say, maintaining eye contact.

"Were you born in the forties?" He smiles.

No, but my roommate was, I think.

"Go on," he encourages. "Give me details. Like how much time do you spend in it? Do you like to cook? What is the essence of your kitchen?" It is the part of the consult where the doctor is now feeling the breasts.

"I don't know. I don't *love* to cook, but I don't mind cooking when I have time. I can make a cheese ball and tacos and I like drinking wine in the kitchen. I dry my hair in it when I drink my coffee in the morning and I don't wash the floor as often as I should. I usually wait until something spills and then I use my socks. I like to sit on the counters or on the stove. I once found a grasshopper in my kitchen."

"Keep going," he says.

"I don't know. I have not one but two tracks of brass lighting and there is an unmarked bag of spice in the cupboard that just sits there year after year and I have various metal lids that are missing their jars and scratched-up sippy cups with rubber liners that smell like condoms."

"Do you ever host parties or do Christmas dinners? Do you like to entertain?"

"Only when forced to."

"All right," he says. "I know the perfect colour for your kitchen."

"Which is . . ."

"White."

"White? Seriously? It took you all that to come up with white? Was it the unidentified bag of spice or the sippy cups?"

"No, no. It was white right after you listed your appliances. You have way too much going on in there."

So you are basically admitting you didn't need to touch the breasts after you drew all over them. "Fine, then tell me about your kitchen," I insist.

"It's a galley. Quite small, really. Walls are grey. Backsplash is made up of mosaic tiles, no border, no cornucopias. Separate dining room. Appliances are stainless steel and bulky. Too big for the space. But there is a window over the sink, which looks out onto the backyard. I do not dry my hair in the kitchen but I've played my guitar in it."

Interesting. I've played the skin flute in mine. Another customer enters the store, a middle-aged woman with a pompadour. I fasten my hospital gown.

"The whites are all on that panel over there," he directs. "You want to go with something warm."

The other customer has a picture of a room I am not able to see, and mulls it over with the paint guy. I stare at the paint guy's sculpted calves. They bulge out to the sides like a pair of fists. He must be a runner. The customer sits down at one of the many workstations as the paint guy begins making recommendations. I continue to watch the paint guy with interest, the way a stalker might. He kind of makes me want to paint my whole house. The other customer thinks they are best friends, but I wait patiently for the paint guy to return to my side and my dilemma, in the meantime not paying much attention to the display of white chips in front of me. I can't tell the warm from the cool. I choose one at random and read the name:

icicle. I jam it back in the slot. Where are the warm colours? Why can't I find little lamb or Bequia sand. Where is hug?

"So how are we doing?" he asks when the other customer releases him.

"Not good," I reply. His presence makes me feel giddy.

"Any of these are good choices," he says, sticking a blue pencil behind his ear. I can faintly smell his deodorant. Gilette, cool wave. We compare samples, breaking when new customers arrive in what seem like ten-minute intervals. I finally settle on a shade, acknowledging even the right white will not change all that is wrong with my kitchen. However its name is fairly disappointing: mayonnaise. Surely the only thing worse than having a yellow kitchen is having a mayonnaise one. Especially mayonnaise that costs fifty dollars a gallon. I debate just spreading Miracle Whip over the walls, but the colour works and it doesn't contain eggs or taste good on a sandwich and at least it's going in the kitchen and not the bedroom.

I look over the panels of colour while the paint guy goes to mix the mayonnaise, picking samples at random and reading their names: Flamingo's Dream, Irish Clover, Dead Salmon.

"Your mayonnaise is ready," the paint guy says, nodding towards the counter.

I shove a handful of colour swatches into my purse and follow him to the back of the store.

"Thanks for your help," I say, handing him my Visa. More customers enter the store but he focuses on me. On my ten freckles. The chicken pox scar on my left upper lip, the jagged neck of my most favourite yellow T-shirt. And my clavicle, which is so touchable. It is perhaps the world's most beautiful clavicle, protruding from my chest like a little floating shelf. Or maybe I'm wrong. Maybe it's my intact earlobes, pierced only once and as soft as a horse's face, or my lashes, which are not particularly long but are curled like a fan of tiny beckoning fingers. I don't know, but I feel like the only colour in the room: Claudia.

"No problem," he says. "Listen, if you ever need help replacing the cornucopias, let me know. I'm fairly decent at tiling."

"Some day," I reply. "They're on my hit list."

He lingers for a moment, and then turns to serve another customer, who can't wait to talk about paint for the bar in her basement. I haul my mayonnaise to the car and place it on the passenger seat.

I get back from the paint store feeling renewed and anxious to get started on the kitchen, but, of course, it will have to wait until after the party.

"Hello!" I call, coming in the front door.

I place the mayonnaise down in the front hall, and I walk through the house looking for my family. They're out on the back deck.

"What are you doing?"

"Gardening." There is dirt in Dad's hair, pink in his cheeks. He wipes his nose with his shirt.

"Where did you get plants?"

"We went down to Canadian Tire."

"With the kids?"

"Yes," he says, proudly.

"Without car seats?" I bite my tongue.

"It's just down the street." He disappears around the side of the house and returns seconds later with an obscure-looking bucket.

"What is that?"

"It's a tomato planter. You hang it up like this and the tomatoes grow downwards. They say they grow bigger this way."

"Thanks, Dad, but I'll probably kill it."

"No, no," he argues. "It's really easy. You don't have to bend down and search for them."

"Is that what it says on the box?"

"Yes."

"Really?"

"It's true. You can do it all standing up."

"Oh, Dad."

"Well I will do it then. I'll look after them."

"It's not that, it's that you believe everything on the box. Pass it to me. 'Eliminate back-breaking work.' That's actually amusing."

"One plant produces thirty pounds of tomatoes."

"It was thoughtful of you to get this. The kids and I will just have to start eating more tomatoes."

"Think of it," he says, "We can make sandwiches or salsa or add them to salads or even just eat them on their own."

"Yes," I reply. "We can."

When I go back inside the house I have a full-blown panic attack. The Topsy Turvy tomato plant is not a nice gesture from father to daughter. The Topsy Turvy is a nice gesture from roommate to roommate. It is like the time Glen moved in his toaster oven because he planned to be around for a while. My father plans to be around for a while. He plans to be around to water and pick the tomatoes standing up and he plans on filling the cupboards with baked beans and Q-tips and change jars featuring quarters with pictures of hockey players and curlers on them. And while he plans on staying for the long haul, I can't call Glen on a whim to watch the kids or fix the dryer.

"Look what we got!" Wes says, kicking his Crocs off at the back door. His hands are behind his back. Joan follows him holding her plant sideways. Dad steps in and rights it.

"Hold it up like this, Joanie." He too is holding a plant.

"What do you have there?"

Wes exclaims, "The Scouts were selling them in front of

Canadian Tire! Grandpa says we can plant them and then eat them later." Then he adds, "They're bean plants."

Of course they are. Each in its own little plastic cup. Each wobbly bean dangling from its own finger-length stem. Green and tiny and full of promise.

A little bit later that afternoon when I dress Joan in fresh clothes, I notice her slide wounds are barely visible, though my tailbone still feels as though it was clubbed. Dad remains in the garden. I take Wes to a friend's house to play and Joan and I go shopping for Glen's party. She is more agreeable on her own. We stop at a Tim's on the way and share a snack pack of Timbits as we grocery shop. I skim over my list, which seems to have ballooned since the night before.

We load up the cart with hummus and pretzels and juice boxes and end up spending almost two hundred dollars, not even including the cake, which I had the foresight to order from a bakery. We pick it up after we're done at the grocery store. It has real icing and costs forty-five dollars.

I remind myself again why I'm doing this. For Wes, for Joan to a certain degree. You celebrate the success of your ex because it is important to your child in the same way you agree to play three hundred rounds of *Cars* bingo or drive around the city looking for the Wiggles Christmas movie. And it's important because sometimes things don't work out, like when you throw your kids down a waterslide or make them eat boiled chicken and Rice Krispies for dinner or you separate from their father.

At home Joan plays with dinosaurs as I put away the groceries. I have an hour to clean before I need to pick up Wes. I chip away at the dried banana on the kitchen floor with a butter knife and clean what's left with a magic eraser. Then I go around and open the windows to let in some fresh air. I don't think I have ever done this before, though it is something my mother practiced religiously and within minutes I understand why. The house feels lighter and renewed, as though it has taken a deep cleansing breath, and somehow I feel lighter and renewed too. Structural yoga.

After I've removed clutter and picked up toys and straightened furniture, Joan asks for a snack, so I spread some peanut butter on a banana. I make a cup of tea in my mother's rooster mug and make a mental list of the only things I still need for the party: a few bottles of wine and a case of beer.

"Put your shoes on, Joan."

"I'm busy."

"Too bad. Only a few hours until Daddy's party."

"Is it his birthday?"

"No, Daddy's birthday is in August."

And then I think, it's April 15th. It's been six months since my mother's birthday party.

Joan looks at me funny.

"We're having the party to celebrate Daddy's artwork."

I wonder if she'll too expect a party, to celebrate her pictures of cat squirrels she's brought home from Turtle Grove.

"Should we have a party for you some time?"

She nods.

"Next time."

I check my watch and tell her to scurry to the car. She obeys and rushes outside. We go the liquor store and then pick up Wes who is no longer wearing socks.

"You must remember where you took them off."

"I don't."

"Just keep them on when you go somewhere to play. Is that so difficult? Which pair were they?"

"The ones with the black toes."

"Wes! Those are the expensive ones," I scold him, feeling genuinely disappointed and pathetic that I'm feeling genuinely disappointed. "Keep them on your feet."

"Is it time for Daddy's party?"

"Almost. Now I spent a lot of time cleaning up the house. Other than the dinosaurs, which are already out, don't make a mess."

Everywhere people are out walking. Getting fresh air. The arms of discarded sweatshirts dangle from their owners' waists. Dogs prance from the ends of their leashes. Kids drive by on bikes that are two sizes too small. If I was smart I would have done a barbecue.

"I'm hungry."

"Now? Didn't you have a snack at Alexander's?"

"No. His mom said not before dinner."

"Well, we'll go to McDonald's."

"Can we go in?"

"No, it has to be drive-thru. We have people coming in less than an hour and I'd like to shower and change."

I pull into the drive-thru and roll down my window in anticipation. Clean the dashboard with my finger.

"That looks like Daddy's car," I note, seeing his old car, his summer car, parked in the lot.

"It is!" Wes confirms enthusiastically.

"How can you tell?"

"Because I can see his jacket in the window."

I shield my eyes from the sun to get a better look. "Would you look at that? You're right, Wes, it is Daddy's car. I remember when Daddy bought that jacket."

"Why?"

"Because I just remember." After the car in front of us lurches forward, I pull one spot closer to the menu. "Your father and I had gone snowboarding on a date and he ran into a tree."

"So did he find the jacket on the tree?"

"No. He ripped his jacket right across the back and that," I say, pointing to the almost neon orange coat spread across Glen's rear windshield, "was the only jacket in his size left on the resort."

"Why are you laughing?"

"I just am." I pull the car ahead again. "What do you want?"

"Chicken and fries."

"How about just the fries? We have tons of food at home; this is just a snack."

"Okay. I'll have fries and a cheeseburger."

I shake my head. "Joan, do you want anything?"

"I want a fish."

"You want a fish?"

"She means a Filet-O-Fish," Wes corrects.

"You want a Filet-O-Fish?" I say, looking at Joan surprised. She nods.

"Since when do you like Filet-O-Fish?"

"That's what Daddy's friend gets all the time. It's a square fish."

"Uncle Teddy?"

"No, Daddy's friend Sonia."

"Sonia. Right."

The speaker squawks, "Welcome to McDonald's can I take your order please?"

"I'll have a fish."

"A fish?"

"A Filet-O-Fish and some fries."

"Did you want the combo?"

"Sure, whatever." I turn in my seat and look at Wes. "Does she order it all the time, like, two times, or like *lots* of times?"

"All the time," Wes stresses. "Like probably ten times."

"How often does Daddy take you to McDonald's?"

Wes shrugs.

"What would you like to drink with that?"

Tequila. Purel. Acid. "Coke."

"Drive through for your total."

"What again does Daddy's friend look like?"

"I don't know."

It is the same response he gives when I ask what he did at school.

"Well is she tall or short or does she have brown hair or . . ."

"There she is! See?"

"Where?"

"Over *there*," he taps at his window.

"Welcome to McDonald's can I take your order?"

"You already took it."

I move forward to pay and pick up my square fish, observing with diligence the scene in my rear-view.

"Is that her?" I ask Wes.

He strains his head. "I can't see anymore."

"Does she wear braids sometimes?"

"Uh-huh."

"How old is she?"

"Maybe twenty years old?" Wes guesses. "Same as Daddy."

"Daddy is thirty-six."

"Then maybe she's thirty-six too."

"Fifty ten hundred."

"Thanks, Joan, that's helpful."

I exchange money for food and drive around the parking

lot, find a spot and turn off the engine to watch from an adequate distance. I dig in the bag and hand the kids each a handful of fries. I lick the salt off my fingers. Sonia opens her door and dumps her purse inside. Glen is standing by her side of the car waiting for something. When she returns to an upright position he kisses her and tugs playfully on her braids. He loves her. My Glen is in love. It changes everything and nothing.

I sink into my seat, restart the car. I feel heavy. Cloaked in emotion. A physical reaction. My shoulders actually slope forward towards the wheel as though I'm wearing one of those protective x-ray vests. I am the guy in the Diet Pepsi ads who wants his old jeans back.

Why would Glen go to McDonald's before the party? Does he think I wouldn't have food? It pisses me off.

"Can I have some more fries?"

I hand the entire bag back to Wes. "Go fish. Fill your boots."

"I didn't want a Filet-O-Fish."

He doesn't know what I mean. I don't know what I mean.

"Just eat the fries, Wes."

He opens the bag and starts stuffing food in his mouth. Joan whines. Stretches her arm towards him. He meets her demands and passes her a few. The car goes quiet. Still.

When we stop at a red light I turn on the radio. Release the brake a bit and inch forward. I collapse into the steering wheel. Listen to the Barenaked Ladies lament about popsicles or grade school or something. By the time the light turns green, I'm crying. Tearless, but with really ugly facial expressions. The kids ask what's wrong and I cover my mouth. Shake my head. Motorists in passing cars notice me. They look over and look over again.

"Wes, undo your seat belt," I say, wiping my nose as we

pull into the driveway. He obeys. I get out of the car, unbuckle Joan, and gesture them both out the same side of the car.

"Go on up to the door," I encourage. "I have to get stuff out of the trunk."

"Can I have my fish?" Joan asks.

"When we get in the house. Go! You're standing in Mommy's way."

We tramp into the house, bags swinging, bottles of wine clinking. Fries drop from the open McDonald's bag leaving a trail to the front door.

"Are you okay, Mommy?"

"Yeah, I'm fine, honey." I help Wes off with his shoes.

"Were you thinking about Grandma?"

"Yep. I was. Just thinking about Grandma."

He hugs me.

"I'm okay," I reassure him. "Should we put on *Ice Age?*"

Wes and Joan both cheer. Joan takes off her Crocs and biffs them across the room.

"All right, we have a party to get ready for."

I set the kids up in front of the TV, give Joan her fish, and begin loading the table with snacks and finger foods. Pretzels, popcorn, Brothers pepperoni. Out back my father removes dandelions from the lawn. This will devastate Joan. The cake has the kitchen smelling like fudge. It reminds me of baking with my mom when I was still small enough to need a chair. I want my mom. She kept her fingernails short and perfectly rounded. She made happy faces with the cloves whenever she baked a ham. She was not angry or bitter or resentful for getting hit with that damn boat. And then I think about Glen. The way he used to line up said cloves on his plate during Easter dinner. The way he shaved his face with one arm behind his back. The poem he wrote in the sympathy card he gave me. Asshole.

I open a bottle of wine. Chateau Grand Paris. From 2006. I take a glass from the display on the table and fill it three quarters full. I lean against the counter, tip my glass up, take too large a sip. It floods the back of my throat.

There's no time to shower, really, so instead I stand in the kitchen staring at my cluttered fridge door. It's a wonder I still know it's yellow under all the drawings and notices from school and appointment cards. I remove the magnets and decide I at least have time for this. I discard anything expired or irrelevant. A coupon for buy one get one free Kraft peanut butter. Layers of monthly calendars from Turtle Grove. A menu from King of Donair.

When I'm done, I've uncovered my mother's funeral bulletin. Such a perfect photo Dad chose. There is light in her eyes, a little curl in her hair, and she is wearing her favourite green sweater. I think I should be sad, that seeing it again should make me sad and I should take it down like the other expired notices. But instead I find myself placing a magnet in each corner of the bulletin, adjusting it so it's neat and straight on the fridge, and I smile. She would want to come to the party.

Acknowledgements

Sincere thanks to the entire Board and staff of Freehand Books, particularly JoAnn McCaig and Barbara Scott for acquiring and supporting *Roost* from pitch to print. My Managing Editor, Kelsey Attard, for her unwavering commitment to this project from proof to promotion and whose every communication was delivered with an infectious optimism. My Editor, Robyn Read, who has been immensely generous with her time, expertise and friendship through multiple drafts of this book, particularly the early days before she parked on my lawn, when the book did not have a plot and ham and cheese croissants hadn't yet been discovered. And yes, we can and we did say *Rainman*. My mentor, Betty Jane Hegerat, for her extraordinary ability to simultaneously deliver praise and critique so comments like "I had no idea what was going on here" came across "this is really good." Thanks for leading and following, but please never "get out of the way." Paul "Coach Q" Quarrington, whose advice and validation through the Humber School for Writers set this entire process into motion. Gwen Davies for being there from the get go as my first writing teacher and facilitator. The Writers Guild of Alberta with support from the Canada Council for the WGA Mentorship Program, which bridged the all important gap between the tenth draft and the publishable manuscript. Todd Babiak for generously reading *Roost* and providing a blurb that somehow makes me feel way cooler than I actually am, and Natalie Olsen for designing the cover and capturing the essence of the book so completely.

To my many friends, clients and family who have supported me as a person through this process whether with their words or through gifts of writing time sans children I am eternally grateful. Special thanks to those who specifically supported me as a writer: Patricia Arab, Melanie Battle, Reta Dennis, Rebecca Gulbransen, Erin Haysom, Tanya Heck, Bianca Johnny, Jennie King, Amanda Maclean, Char Martin, Jesse Wallace, Kelly Weedon, Chas Young. My one and only Halifax writing group: Mary Clancy, Dennis Earle, Nancy Newcomb, Atulya Saxena, and Mary-Evelyn Ternan. My big sisters, "Amy the Great" Weedon for cheerleading and Amanda Brazil for laughing at my jokes. My father, Peter Weedon, for his encouragement and support and my mother Diane Wallace, my original mentor and editor, my always mother, for her unparalleled support and guidance. This book is your success too. To my three babes: Pippa, Hugo and Odessa for keeping me grounded and inspired with your wild and wooly ways and tolerating me on the days I was up writing at five in the morning and was an asshole by eight at night. To my husband, Dave Bryan, my first fan, for accepting me unconditionally. Through open cupboard doors, small portions, and jackets on the floor, you never doubted this would happen. You are one cool accountant.

Last, thanks be to God. How great thou art, how great thou art.

Ali Bryan is a personal trainer who grew up in Halifax and attended high school in Sackville, New Brunswick. She is a graduate of St. Mary's University and completed a graduate certificate in creative writing from the Humber School for Writers under the tutelage of Paul Quarrington. She was a finalist in the 2010 CBC Canada Writes literary contest for her essay "Asshole Homemaker" and a bronze medalist in the 2012 Canada Writes Literary Triathlon. Ali lives in Calgary with her husband and three children. Her real name is Alexandra. *Roost* is her first novel.